Where the Hell is Ivy Dell?

Indie Sparks

Twice Shy Publishing

Book Cover by Indie Sparks

Edited by Beth Hudson, Ink

Contents

For Everyone Who:

- Daydreams about running away for a few months

- Makes wishes on falling stars

- Has ever fucked on the first date – or would if they could
go back in time

Get in all you daydreamers, wish-makers,
and reckless fuckers!
We're going to the desert.

I'd like to extend thanks in advance to the inevitable reviewer
who will rate this book one-star and say there is too much sex in
it—unless you slut shame Ivy in the process, in which case I wish
upon you an incurable UTI.
Bless your heart.

From Indie

A Quick Note Before You Begin

This is book 1 of a 4-book novella series, but it can be read as a stand alone.

Though all the threads will not be wrapped up in any of the first 3 books, I do take care not to leave the books with major cliffhangers. There will be some questions left unanswered, but my intention is to leave you wanting more, not wanting to throw the book (or your reading device - yikes!) across the room.

I think a little time with Jensen Stinger is worth a few lingering questions. Happy Reading!

SETTING: A Cheery Yellow, Three-Bedroom Cottage in a Quaint Texas Beach Town

SEASON: Tourists Being Broiled Alive on Satan's Ballsack / Locals in Hiding

I KNEW THE DAY would come that Mom and I would have to go through Gran's things. I've imagined it in my head at least a dozen times since her diagnosis. The word terminal still makes me think of an airport, but the word fly? That's forever tied to Gran.

It's what she always said she would do—not die, only fly away. When I was a little girl, it seemed magical that our time in this life would be done, and we would simply fly away to our next adventure.

Gran flew two weeks ago, and it still feels too soon to be going through this stuff. But Mom insisted today was the day, so here we are, lugging boxes down from a humid attic in August. Insanity.

The grief hits her like a tidal wave every morning, and I don't want to make it worse for her, but I still feel like we could've waited a while longer. I sit cross-legged on the rug and face the stacks of boxes, all full of things Gran couldn't let go of. She was sentimental, but so far, this looks like mostly financial paperwork.

People don't save old bank statements out of sentimentality. They do it because they were told maintaining physical documents was vitally important. For all her ability to change, Gran didn't trust digital record keeping. I don't know how she could have this much paperwork. She didn't own a business. Well, okay, she technically did, but not one that required an excess of paperwork. You want to paint angels; you paint angels. No articles of incorporation or trust documents required.

She sold her artwork in a local gallery, refusing to even consider having her own website. The internet had no soul; it was no place for her abstract angels.

Never mind the dozens of sites I showed her belonging to artists whose work she genuinely admired. Gran was never one to be swayed once she formed an opinion.

There is no pressing estate to settle. Mom's an only child, and she and Gran bought the house together. It's hers now. It's not like she has to sell it to divvy up the equity between heirs. A zap zings at the base of my spine and zips straight up to my skull. I drop the lid I've just removed from a dusty box.

"Mom, are you selling the house?"

"We bought it twenty years ago, honey. The market is at an all-time high, and I don't need all this space anymore. You've moved out, and now Mom's gone. I'm thinking of getting a nice, two-bedroom condo. Right on the beach. No upkeep. You'd still have a room to crash in when you come over for movie-and-wine night."

"Surrounded by tourists at every turn. You'd be miserable. Please don't make a decision this big yet. Give yourself some time."

"That's just it, honey. We always think we have more time than we do." She pulls a stack of paperwork from a box and flips through it before she stands. "Let me get a trash bag. I'm sure that's where most of this stuff is headed."

I blink back tears. This is the house where I grew up. We moved here when I was seven. There was a string of shitty apartments before this place, but this is the only home I really remember. All my memories live in these walls. I don't want strangers living in our house.

Mom was young when she had me, and my dad wasn't in the picture, aside from the wild stories I heard about him growing up. Supposedly, he was a seven-foot-tall, red-haired magician who worked in Las Vegas, and the moment he heard he was going to be a father, he did the ultimate disappearing act.

Who was he really? Who the fuck knows? Mom and Gran obviously never wanted me to know. Hence the ridiculous tales they wove about him. I mean, people say I'm tall at five-ten, but there's nothing extraordinary about my height, nothing to indicate one of my parents is the tall of tall-tales variety. *Seven feet.*

And sure, there aren't any red-haired relatives visible in our generations going back as far as photography, despite our last name being McAdams, so maybe my father did have red hair, but I never wanted for him. If height and hair color were all he ever gave me, that was fine with me.

The women who raised me were all I ever needed.

They both sacrificed for me. I know they did. If Mom wants a condo, she deserves a condo. I imagine what Gran would say about that, and her voice rings clearly in my ear.

*It's good to have homes of a
different sort throughout your*

> *life. You get to thinkin' you
> can only survive in one kind of
> place, and before you know it,
> that'll become your truth. You'll
> lose a lot of things in this life,
> Ivy Dell, but don't you ever lose
> your ability to adapt. Change is
> good, even if it sometimes feels
> bad at the outset. You go with
> the wind, grow wherever you
> land next.*

I laugh as I set aside a stack of bank statements postmarked from 2016. It seems like that's all this box holds, just as I suspected. Dumping it out onto the rug, I do a cursory fan-through with my hands, seeing nothing but the bank's return address on every envelope.

Except one.

There, peeking out from the plain white envelopes, is a light blue one with a handwritten return address. A letter from someone named Petra. No last name, but none needed.

I heard plenty of stories about Gran's good friend Petra when I was growing up.

Petra was one of the eclectic residents of Ivydell, the hippie-dippy little enclave of artists and mystics Gran loved so dearly that she convinced my mother to name me after the place. A place my mother lived until the age of thirteen, though she never professed the same level of love for it as Gran. In her defense, it was supposedly in the ass-end of a west Texas desert.

I say supposedly because most of the stories sounded so far-fetched, there's always been a part of me that questioned if it was ever real. It couldn't have existed the way Gran portrayed it, but some of Mom's stories were pretty unbelievable, too, though she mostly complained about how hard it was to adjust to living in a normal city after Ivydell disbanded.

She never attended public school, or any official school, but she was on grade level academically. Socially? That was apparently a whole other story. None of her classmates saw herbalists before doctors or knew which phase of the moon to charge their crystals under. Eventually, she learned to play volleyball and caught up on current music and TV shows, but she never truly felt like she fit in her post-Ivydell world until after high school.

It's no wonder she threw herself into her coursework in college, pregnant and all. Did I mention she was eighteen when she lost her virginity to the towering magician? She found more than she bargained for on the Vegas Strip on her eighteenth birthday—if my whole origin story is to be believed.

At any rate, nursing school brought her up to speed with the real world, crash-course style. But being an emergency room nurse is her calling. I'll always believe that.

Where is she with that trash bag? Probably taking a break to cry in the kitchen. She's still trying not to do it in front of me.

I should probably save the letter from Petra until she's back. We can read it together.

But the last thing she may want right now is a journey back to Ivydell. The postmark on the letter is older than the other envelopes in the box, twenty-years-old to be exact. Why would Gran have stuffed it in between all these old bank statements?

It's clearly been opened before, but I guess the humidity partially resealed it at some point. I slide my finger under the dried-out adhesive on the envelope. The flap pops open immediately. I unfold the single page.

Dearest Patrice,

It's finally happening! We've won the rights to OUR land! We are free to return to Ivydell. I promised you I'd never give up the fight. Those oil and gas fuckers are out!

Come home, Patrice! Ivydell is waiting.

And so am I.

All my love,

Petra

Ivydell was the great love of Gran's life. She would've jumped at the chance to go back. Why didn't she?

I look up to see Mom leaning against the arched opening between the kitchen and living room. "What are you reading?"

"It's a letter from Petra."

"Oh. I'd imagine she has a box full of those."

"This one was in a box of bank statements. Almost like she'd hidden it there, Mom. Did you know Ivydell was resettled?"

"What? When?"

She steps closer, and I hand her the envelope. "Two decades ago, according to the postmark on this letter."

"This is the same month we bought the house." She sits on the couch and reads Petra's words several times over. "I regret an awful lot about the way she raised me, but I always knew I was loved. She knew I'd never raise you there, and she'd have never left us."

"I always believed going back to Ivydell was what she wanted most in the whole world."

"What she wanted most in this world was to be with us, sweetheart. Her family." She wipes her eyes and shrugs. "That's a mother's and a grandmother's love."

I watch as Mom's eyes mist over again, and I know I'm supposed to be grateful to Gran for loving us like that, but it makes me angry.

All I can think is that's just another level of emotional manipulation that gets put on the shoulders of women. With all the ground we've gained, it's still supposed to be honorable when we put ourselves second. That's bullshit.

She should've felt free to go back to her little west Texas utopia and paint swirling angels taking flight from opening cactus blooms and tumbling in the cold winter breath of howling coyotes.

She should've been free to fly while she was still alive. Not shackled by love.

Ivy

Six Months Later

"For the last time, Mom, I have to do this. I need to see Ivydell for myself."

She yanks one of my bags from the hatch before I can close it. It's the smallest of all my bags. I could probably live without it, but I can't just drive away from her when she's so upset.

"This isn't a day trip, Ivy! You're going to the other side of the state! It's nine hours away! And you don't even know what you're headed into!"

"Mom, please stop yelling. Your neighbors are going to report you to the board."

"Let them. I hate living here, anyway. We should buy the house back, me and you."

She clutches my weekender like it's an infant I'm trying to abduct.

"You love your condo. And we cannot buy our old house back. It's not even for sale."

I tug on the strap, and she gives up the bag with a huff. "I could come with you."

"No, you can't. The hospital is short-staffed as it is. You can't take off on a spontaneous sabbatical."

"You're doing it."

"I'm going to be working remotely. No one's life depends on my presence."

"Thank goodness. You can barely take care of yourself. Just because it's a desert doesn't mean it won't get cold. It's February. You don't even own a proper coat. I know you don't."

I drop the bag between us and wrap my arms around her. "I will wear layers. Three sweaters and two pairs of pants every day. If I leave now, it will still be daylight when I get to Ivydell. If I leave *now*."

My arms go slack, and I step away from her, toss my bag back into the car, and close the hatch.

"Your gran built that place up in your mind, honey. You're going to be so disappointed."

"I don't have any grand illusions. One hundred acres with nothing but adobe casitas and dirt roads. Thirty miles from the nearest city. Not a grocery store in sight. No restaurant delivery services. I know. But there are people living there. It's not a ghost town."

"It's full of ghosts, Ivy. Those people are all trying to outrun a troubled past or mourning an expired dream. All you're going to find are a bunch of people who are out of touch with reality and scared of the world. And scorpions. Did I mention the scorpions?"

"So many times. I love you. I'll be back in a few months." I don't know how to explain that it may be ghosts I'm hoping to find. All I know is everything here makes me sad and restless and angry, and there has to be a reason I can't get Ivydell out of my head. Like it's calling to me day and night.

A seagull drops lower, flying by to see me off. With a rush of emotion, I realize I'm actually going to miss these squawking scavengers. I almost wish I had a French fry to toss up as a parting gift.

And then the bon voyage bird shits right in the center of my back windshield.

Mom and I both jump aside and then burst into laughter. I slide behind the wheel before she has time to get upset again, roll down the window, and wave as I pull away.

"I'll text with updates every time I stop for gas or food," I yell.

"With a picture! So I'll know it's really you!" she yells back.

My back windshield wiper works double-time all the way to the ferry landing. I'm the last car loaded. I walk to the side to watch the waves as we float away from the island. A pod of dolphins plays in the wake. I'm definitely going to miss those. No dolphins in Ivydell, I guess. Just ghosts.

And scorpions.

Ivy

On the Road

ROAD TRIPS WITH FRIENDS have always been my favorite things, but I've been looking forward to this solo journey. Me and the open road. Alone with my thoughts. And a bag full of clearance after-Valentine's-Day candy.

In my head, this was going to be a peaceful time to make plans and consider my future, but so far, it's been an hour of heavy traffic where I can't focus on anything other than survival, followed by a string of small-town speed traps where I have to keep my eyes peeled for those damn hidden speed limit signs, then another round of traffic and road ragers—wash, rinse, repeat.

Who can think of anything other than driving under these conditions?

I suppose the argument could be made that driving is exactly what I should be thinking about when I'm behind the wheel, but is the occasional hypnotic stretch of road really too much to ask?

Throughout all this driving while thinking about driving, my *check engine* light has been playing peek-a-boo. It's been doing it for a while now. It stays on just long enough for me to start to panic, and then it blinks off again.

I'm choosing to believe it's a loose connection. Maybe the bulb is going out? I hope that's all it is because I'm approaching the last leg of the drive. The land of stoplights and Starbucks is already behind me. I haven't seen a Buc-ee's in ages.

No man's land.

Plenty of windmills, though.

The huge white blades cartwheeling across the sky are hypnotic in their own way. Lots of time to think out here. I wonder if Ivydell will welcome me with open arms. Patrice's granddaughter returning to the motherland and all. My namesake even.

Petra was happy to rent me a casita for a few months. All it took was one letter, and then we handled the details via email. She didn't even ask for a deposit, just my word that I was coming. I get the impression she's the de facto mayor of Ivydell, though it's not an actual city, more of a . . . hamlet? Ranch? Compound?

A convenience store with two gas pumps appears on the horizon. I still have a little over half a tank, but I'm realizing now I didn't ask a lot of questions that are starting to seem important the closer I get to my destination. How far is the nearest gas station from Ivydell? How far will I be from a hospital? Why am I just now wondering these things?

I pull into the parking lot. It never hurts to top off the tank. May as well grab some more snacks while I'm here.

The guy behind the counter looks to be about nineteen and like he'd rather be anywhere else in the world. He doesn't even look up when I ask about the restrooms, just gestures vaguely toward the back of the store.

When I set my bottle of water and bag of chips on the counter, he finally glances up at me. His demeanor is suddenly friendly. "Where ya headed?"

"To Ivydell."

"Where?"

"Ivydell."

"Is that a college or something?"

"No. It's where I'm going to live."

"Oh. It's the name of some apartments?"

"It's houses, like a neighborhood. A big one, a hundred acres."

"What city is it in?"

"Um . . . it's not really in a city."

"Is it in New Mexico?"

"It's in Texas."

"Are you sure? You're almost out of Texas. I've never heard of any place around here called Ivydell."

"It sounds strange, but now that I think about it, I guess it's sort of exclusive. There's no big sign or anything. And you kind of have to be invited to live there. It's surrounded by a fence in some places, a wall in others. The residents are intentionally secluded, so it makes sense that if you aren't a part of it, you might not realize it's there."

"Pretty sure you're describing either a mental hospital or a prison. And you don't really seem like you belong in either one."

"I don't belong in either one. It's hard to explain."

"Listen, my uncle is the sheriff. If you're in some kind of trouble—"

"I am not in any kind of trouble. Please, just ring up my stuff so I can get back on the road."

"The road to Ivydell."

"Exactly."

"Whatever you say."

He's looking at me like I said I'm following the yellow brick road to Oz. Like Ivydell doesn't exist. But it does. I've heard stories about it my whole life. I've seen pictures!

"You are without a doubt the prettiest woman who's ever come in here. I knew you were probably headed someplace else, but . . ." He trails off as if he knows he shouldn't finish that sentence.

"It's a real place."

"Okay. Well, I hope you're happy there."

I grab my chips and water. "Thanks. I hope you're happy here."

"Nobody is happy here."

The sadness in his voice wrecks me. For a scant moment, I almost wish I could take him with me to Ivydell. Surely, he deserves more than this. But he's grown. He'll have to find his own happiness.

The bells on the door jangle as I push it open, and the young man's voice stops me in my tracks.

"What's your name?"

"Ivy."

"Right. I feel like I should've guessed that. Can I get your number?"

"You think I'm batshit bonkers, don't you?"

"Maybe a little."

"Then why do you want my number?"

"Because you're interesting. And drop dead gorgeous."

"And entirely too old for you." I smile at him before I step past the door, letting it sweep shut behind me.

A gust of wind sucks the door back open a few inches, and I hear him yell, "I'm older than I look!"

My eyeballs feel like they've been sandblasted by the time I get back to my car. The wind continues to whip while I sit blinking for a few moments, wondering how someone ends up in a place like this. The entire population was probably born here.

And then there's me, traveling across the entire state to live in a walled-off compound that the locals have never even heard of. Who wouldn't think I was a little nuts?

I knew I was going to have to turn onto a dirt road to find Ivydell, but when I reach the spot, I put my car in park and stare straight ahead. There are no houses in sight, not even the fence, just a whole hell of a lot of nothing, punctuated by a lone mesa in the distance.

Ivydell lies well beyond that mesa. Everything is exactly as Petra described it, but I can't help second-guessing myself. It feels like once I take this road less traveled, there will be no turning back, which is silly. I can turn back anytime.

My front tires glide off the asphalt onto the packed dirt as if they've been down this road a thousand times before.

The way curves and suddenly, the mesa is behind me. It doesn't get any closer, just remains surrounded by wavering vapors in a different direction now. But something new is coming into view, something tall and dark. It's the fence; it has to be.

After miles and miles and hours and hours of increasing trepidation, the excitement I felt when I set out on this journey returns. It fizzes in my core, making me bounce behind the wheel.

I see the huge rock with the bear painted on it. Bear rock. That means the entrance is just up ahead. My car slows. It takes a few beats for me to realize I've let my foot off the gas. A pair of hawks swoop past my windshield like a welcoming committee. I should probably be wary of birds getting too close to my car after the parting gift from the seagull this morning.

Are hawks a good omen or a bad one? Is this a warning?

Ridiculous. It's the desert. Hawks are common here. As common as dirt. And scorpions. I shake my head and press the accelerator, dismissing all my wildlife concerns.

The rusty iron gates are open just like Petra said they'd be. I drive through, slowing again to take in the adobe casitas squatting like toy houses at random intervals. The first building I reach is the community center, also just as Petra described it. I know it serves as a coffee shop, meeting place, dance hall, pretty much any purpose that requires a communal location.

Next is a set of two small buildings connected by a large open but covered bay that serves as the community's service hub. One building says Mechanic on the front and the other says Plumbing & Electrical. It looks like there is a junkyard of sorts behind them. There are two trucks parked in the covered space in between, one regular pickup and one that looks more like a service vehicle with toolboxes and a welding machine in the bed.

My foot falls like lead onto my brake pedal. Holy mother of scorpions. Where did he come from?

And why isn't he wearing a shirt? Is he staring at me?

Or am I staring at him?

Ivy

Upon Arrival

PETRA DID NOT MENTION the abs. I mean, the arms. I mean, the man.

This man with the abs and the arms under such perfectly taut bronze skin. He's walking toward my car. I should woll down the rindow. Roll, not woll. Roll it down. The glass. Window. I know it goes down, but I don't remember how exactly to make that happen.

He's right next to my car now. His hand is making a rolling motion, which is causing his biceps to move up and down. Up and down. Pulling my eyes. Up. Down.

Then he says, loudly enough for me to hear him through the glass, "Push the button."

Right. Fuck. The button. That's how it works.

I fumble, pushing the wrong one first, but I get it on the second try. His hair is the honeyed russet shade of the paler adobe shop buildings, while mine is a closer match to the darker rust-red cottages I've not yet reached. I'm tall, but he's taller. He's broad where I'm slim. And sweet Jesus, why can't I stop chronicling our every physical comparison? "Hi," I manage.

"Hi," he says in a voice that's deep, practically booming after mine came out so thready and weak. "Are you lost?"

"I don't think so. This is Ivydell, right?"

He looks taken aback that I actually know where I am, that I'm here on purpose. "This is indeed Ivydell."

His hand encroaches through my window as if he might brush my hair off my cheek or run his thick fingers through my long tresses. Maybe clench his fist and pull ever so slightly, hard enough to tilt my head back for a . . .

Oh, shit. He's extending it for a handshake. The man is attempting to shake my hand. I hurriedly grasp it, hoping my micro-fantasy didn't translate. "Hi," I say again, with a smidge more confidence this time. "I'm Ivy. Ivy Dell McAdams."

Why did I give him my whole name like I'm here to apply for a job?

"Your name is Ivy Dell?"

"Yes. Petra is expecting me. I'm renting a cottage from her for a few months."

"I don't believe you."

"It's true. I can pull up our emails on my phone. I'm going to be staying in Sparrow's Song." The casitas all have names instead of house numbers.

His strong hand releases mine. "Your name. I don't believe that's actually your name."

"Oh, well, I can definitely prove that." I rummage around in my purse for my wallet, and flip it open to reveal my driver's license behind its little clear pocket. "Here."

He peers at it like he's an officer who's pulled me over. My eyes instinctively fall to his hip to check for a pair of cuffs on a utility belt. None to be seen. No cuffs, no belt. Just soft, worn denim hugging his hips, hanging onto the sculpted V that defines the sides of his waist as it narrows, the black band of boxer briefs peeking out above his belt loops.

I look up to find his gray-green eyes tracking mine, but not before I catch sight of the scorpion at the base of his neck, its tail curved upward from the crook at the left side of his collarbone. God, the way I want to trace that scorpion with my tongue.

He not only needs to put on a shirt STAT, it needs to be a turtleneck.

"Huh, I'll be damned," he quips. "Welcome to Ivydell, Ivy Dell."

"Just Ivy. No need for the middle name. I don't know why I introduced myself that way."

"Pleasure to meet you. I'm Jensen."

"Is that your real name?"

He pulls his wallet from his back pocket and takes out his license.

"Jensen James Stinger," I read aloud. "Your last name is Stinger? I guess that explains the tattoo."

"What do you mean?"

I touch my neck in the spot where his scorpion sits. "You have the scorpion there, so I thought . . . when I saw your last name . . . I-I just assumed—"

His laughter is cocky and unfairly sexy. "Yes, Ivy Dell. It's the reason for the tattoo. I get called Stinger a lot more often than Jensen."

"Well, I won't be calling you Stinger. And you can't call me Ivy Dell. It's just Ivy."

"All right then, Just Ivy, do you need me to show you how to find Sparrow's Song?"

Looking through my windshield, I'm shocked to see that a thin coat of dust has already settled over the glass. The hazy view is clear enough to get me to my casita, though. Petra gave me detailed directions. I definitely do not need him to lead the way.

"Yeah, that would be great. Thanks."

Jensen

At First Sight

I CHECK MY REARVIEW again to be sure she's really following me. What the hell are the odds a woman named Ivy Dell would show up here? No way. Too on the nose. She's up to something.

A reporter, maybe? But nothing goes on out here that would interest anybody who didn't live here. Ivydell is not a place anyone chooses for excitement. People come here for the exact opposite.

There aren't any newcomers likely to be hiding from the law. It's possible a few of the old-timers could be, but if nobody has come for them in the past, why now?

It might take me a minute, but I'll figure out Just Ivy's angle.

I'm not an idiot, though. I realize the fact that she looks like a fucking goddess is going to make it hard to maintain a safe distance. That red hair and those full lips. And I've only seen her sitting in her car. When I get a view of the complete package, I'll probably sprain something. Hell, just staring at her long, elegant fingers had my cock jumping in my jeans, aching to feel her soft hands on it.

She was checking me out, too. The attraction's mutual, but the last damn thing I need to do is act on it.

Not with her gorgeous face and body, and that quick wit I can already see, lurking just under the surface, ready and able to challenge me. It's been a long time since I even thought about . . .

Nope, not thinking about it now either. Getting laid hasn't been a problem since I moved here, and I don't need to turn it into one.

I don't do emotions, and she doesn't strike me as the type of woman who does anything purely physical. She's made of complications. Baggage.

Unless she really is here looking for nothing more than a temporary change of scenery. She said she was only renting the place from Petra for a few months.

But her name is Ivy Dell? Bullshit. She blew her cover before she even got started. I don't care what her license says. She wouldn't be the only person living out here under an assumed identity.

My truck rolls to a stop in front of her temporary home. She turns onto the dirt driveway and immediately hops out of her car.

Well, I definitely called that correctly. Watching her long legs and curvy ass as she walks over the stepping stones to the front door has my dick throbbing again. She could give a man a heart attack in that cropped sweatshirt and those tight black leggings.

Whoever invented cropped sweatshirts and sweaters either deserves an ass kicking or an award. Why is that so damn sexy? It doesn't even make sense.

I shouldn't follow her inside.

But it would be a dick move to just drive off. Shit.

"Welcome to your new home, sweet home." I step inside, but leave the front door open. She flits around like a hummingbird.

"It's so cute! Look at this tiny fridge!"

"Yeah, it's adorable."

"I can't believe I have a king-sized bed. I've never had a bed this big. I can spread out for days. Starfish every night!"

Maybe we should go back to talking about the fridge.

She falls onto her back on the mattress and starts to gyrate and stretch. Fuck me. I don't know what she's supposed to be doing, but watching her writhe on the bed like that is doing things to me.

"I'll get out of your way and let you get settled."

Why is she staring at me like that?

"You seriously still haven't put a shirt on? Do you ever wear one?"

I'd literally forgotten I wasn't wearing one. Painfully aware of it now. "I forgot to put it back on before we drove over here. It's still in the shop."

"You should keep an extra in your truck."

"Good idea."

"Because, honestly . . ." she starts, but pauses as if her breath has been stolen. "That's absolutely the most beautiful thing I have ever seen."

I follow her gaze out the patio doors. The sun is setting over the desert. I smile, remembering the first time I saw it. "It's pretty damn breathtaking, isn't it?"

"Pictures don't do it justice."

"Not even close."

We step out onto her back patio. The only fence in Ivydell is the one around the perimeter, so it's easy to find an unobstructed view. The sky is all bright pinks and tangerine. Within minutes, streaks of violet and copper will start to spread.

I know I should leave, but the pull to watch her beautiful face fill with awe as she watches the splendor is too strong. A warm breeze blows over us, and the sweet scent of her hair wafts in my direction. It's not overwhelming, not fake sweet like candy or fruit, but soft and fresh, like Petra's herb garden.

A prairie dog sits up at the edge of the yard, and Ivy squeaks with delight. "He's so precious!"

"They're a menace. You'll see." But then, I realize she probably won't see the nuisance of them. "Actually, I guess you won't be here long enough to plant anything. Maybe they'll always be cute to you."

"They will one thousand percent always be cute to me." She turns to face me. "Are there really seventeen species of scorpions here?"

"I have no idea. I've only ever seen the ones that look like this." I point to my neck. "Sometimes a little bigger, but nothing exotic."

"Have you ever been stung?"

"Plenty of times. Hurts like hell, but you won't die. Unless you're allergic. You're not, are you?"

"How would I know?" She shrugs. "I guess I'll find out if I get stung."

"Most people aren't. I'm sure you'll be fine."

"Maybe I'll get lucky and won't ever get stung."

"Anything's possible."

That look in her eyes makes me feel instantly more exposed, way beyond being shirtless. It's past time for me to go.

I'm halfway to the door when I realize she probably doesn't have any groceries. Who knows what she was expecting to find here? The nearest grocery store is over half an hour away, and the closest restaurant is the same. "Have you eaten dinner? There's nowhere close to get food, but I was about to put some burgers on the grill. I can feed you if you need to eat."

Wow, so hospitable. I wanted to make it clear I wasn't asking her to come over for dinner like it was a date, but I didn't mean to be a complete ass about it.

"I'm supposed to let Petra know when I'm settled. I think she's feeding me tonight."

"Cool. I thought she might be. Just didn't want to leave you hungry."

"Were you planning to put on a shirt if I'd taken you up on the offer?"

"Would it have bothered you if I hadn't?"

Her eyes rake over my chest in a way that makes me want to steal her away before Petra has a chance to cook her dinner. To call dibs, say I asked her first.

But put on a shirt? Not a fucking chance after she looked at me like that.

"It's impolite not to put on a shirt for dinner."

"I don't worry too much about manners at this point in my life."

"That's a shame."

"Not when you're shameless."

Our eyes lock, and there's no way she's not feeling the same electric charge that's running up my spine. I turn on my heels and get the hell out of there.

Ivy

By the Light of Day

I DON'T THINK OF myself as overly sensitive, but it was hard not to take it personally last night when Petra brought dinner by and dropped it off. Her last email had said she wanted to have me over to her place for dinner and to get to know each other.

She claimed she was so excited about having Patrice's granddaughter here. But when I texted to say I had arrived safely, her return message was curt.

At least dinner was good. And she brought me sheets and the most sumptuous fluffy down comforter and pillows, but it still didn't feel very welcoming. She offered a harried excuse of not feeling well and not wanting to get me sick, but I didn't buy it. It was obvious she didn't want to be around me at all.

If I'm being honest, it made me regret turning down Jensen's burger offer. I might've reached out to him if he'd given me his number. He got out of here in a hurry, too.

Could I really make such a bad first impression and have gone this long without knowing it?

There's nothing left for me to unpack. I guess it's a good day to drive around and explore.

My heart jumps when someone knocks on my door. I'm hopeful it's Petra, feeling better and ready to visit with me for a while. After all, I came here to understand why Gran hadn't moved back to Ivydell when the opportunity arose.

Mom can choose to believe it was because she loved us too much to leave us, but I'm certain there has to be more to it. And I think if anyone knows the underlying truth, it's probably Petra.

I swing the door wide, but I don't recognize the woman standing there. She's much younger than Petra. Her hair is a thick mass of wild dark curls, and her eyes are so blue they don't look real. A heavily tattooed arm juts out, offering her hand. Lots of handshakers here, apparently. "Hi, I'm your neighbor, Josephine."

"Hi. I'm Ivy."

"Welcome to nowhere. Thought I'd introduce myself since we're the only two who live on this row."

That can't be right. There are four other houses. She watches me look up and down the street. "All empty," she says. "Hell, my place is empty three days a week, but I'm usually around Monday afternoon through Thursday morning before I head out again."

"Are you a musician?"

"Tattoo artist. I work at a shop in Albuquerque Friday through Sunday. Unless I'm at a show."

"Isn't that a long commute?"

"A little over four hours." She shrugs. "There's no traffic. I like the drive."

"You have a place there, too?"

"Yeah, I like to split my time between civilization and here. It works for me. When I'm there, I go nonstop. When I'm here, I stop."

"So, four nights a week, I'll be the only one staying on this whole street?"

"Don't worry. Stinger lives up front, and he keeps an eye on who comes and goes. And then there's Petra and Cujo and Dice and—"

"I'm sorry. Did you say Cujo?"

"Yeah, big, burly biker dude. You can't miss him. Or his loud-ass Harley, but he's cool. Disappears for weeks on end sometimes, but when he's around, nobody who doesn't belong here will be around for long. But it's really never been a problem, either. People don't just stumble into this place. We're off the beaten path by design."

I'm still trying to wrap my head around having a neighbor who goes by Cujo. "Why does he disappear for weeks at a time?"

"That's none of my business. Or yours."

"Got it. You mentioned someone named Dice. Is he a big, burly, vanishing biker too?"

"Nope. Tall and lanky. Pretty much only leaves when he's headed for a tournament or a weekend in Vegas. Professional poker player. He shares more about his life than Cujo, but the general rule around here is not to ask questions. People will tell you what they want you to know."

"If he plays poker, why is his nickname Dice instead of something to do with cards?"

"He's never explained it."

"And you've never asked."

"You catch on quick."

"I met Jensen already."

"Good for you." She smiles past me at my still messy bed.

"Oh, no. I didn't mean it like that. He showed me to my place. That's all."

"I didn't ask. And you don't owe me an explanation."

"Right."

Dammit. Now, I want to know what her relationship with Jensen is. She calls him Stinger, which doesn't seem intimate at all, but then again, she seems like she probably prefers using nicknames. Not that it's not his real name, but I've never called a man by his last name. I didn't even do that with guy friends growing up.

But I'm not supposed to ask. Maybe she'll volunteer the info if I keep talking to her.

"Is that it? Are there only the six of us living in Ivydell?"

"Oh, no. There are twenty houses in total. With you here now, eighteen are occupied, but some of the residents aren't here much in the off season. And some just prefer to keep to themselves. I lived here for two years before I met Shadow."

"The off season?"

"Winter can get pretty brutal. But spring and summer are amazing. The desert is in bloom and the artists are all in residence. The spirit sisters come back and book sessions. For them, you see visitors come and go at odd hours, but they always let Stinger and Petra know if they're seeing late night clients."

"I'm afraid to ask."

"They're mediums. Twins. Alma and Elma. They're in their seventies, but you'd never know it. You'll see them out and about during the day, especially early mornings. It's when they take walks. They nap in the middle of the day, so don't disturb them. The spirits show up in the evening, and that's when their clients come."

"The mediums and artists sound more like the Ivydell my Gran always talked about. Is Shadow an artist?"

"No. He's not a fan of the festival or the shoppers and seekers who come and go during the season. He doesn't interact much. Comes and goes without anyone seeing him most of the time. Stinger says he checks in with him on his way in and out, but the rest of us rarely get a glimpse of him."

"Is he here now?"

"He might be. His house is the farthest back on the property. If you don't see him driving in or out, it's hard to know."

"What does he do?"

"He's never said. Stinger and Cujo ride back and check on his place, and him when he's around."

"Do you want to go to the store with me?"

"Sure," she says. "I could actually use some supplies. Thanks."

My tires kick up dust as we make our way back to the pavement. I look around for landmarks, but everything looks the same. It's a good thing that mesa is there. A person could get well and truly lost out here, which seems to be the point for some of Ivydell's residents.

"Will you be here for the festival?" Josephine asks.

"When is it?"

"First weekend in April."

"Yeah, I will be, but I don't know anything about it."

She gives me the full rundown. Ivydell charges admission at the front gate, and tourists stream through, buying art and taking pictures like we live in a damn theme park. But the money from the entry fees goes into a general maintenance fund, so the inconveniences are worth it.

"Is Jensen an artist?"

"No, he's a mechanic. And a plumber and an electrician. Pretty much anything that needs to be fixed, he's your guy."

My check engine light flickers as if it's responding to the news. Josephine sees it and smiles. "Better tell Stinger about that. You don't want to break down out here."

She's right. I don't. But I'm not sure I trust Jensen under my hood either. My car's still under warranty. I probably shouldn't let some random dude mess around with my parts.

"What's your opinion on the prairie dogs?" I ask.

"Don't get close enough to let one bite you. They carry the fucking plague. Don't be fooled by their curious little faces. Damn, if you like those rodents, you're really going to be a sucker for the chipmunks."

I didn't expect her to be so anti-cute-little-creatures. "There are honest to God chipmunks here?"

"They're hibernating now, but they'll be all over soon enough. Little shits will eat everything you plant, and the wires in your car. You gotta use peppermint oil."

"How?"

"Just sprinkle it all around under the hood. They don't like the smell."

"Where do I get it?"

"Petra makes it, but I've got extra. I'll give you a vial."

"Thanks. Got any scorpion repellant?"

"You need lavender oil for those little hellfire bastards."

"Does Petra make that, too?"

"Of course. She has every essential oil you could ever need. She's an herbalist."

"And these oils work?"

"Like a charm."

"What if I need an actual charm? Do we have a resident witch, too?" I laugh.

She doesn't.

"Maybe there's a little witch in all of us." Her expression is unreadable, but I'm pretty sure I've offended her. I don't know if that means she identifies as a witch, or just that she thinks I'm a closed-minded outsider who doesn't belong here.

I feel like everyone is a little suspicious of me so far, even Petra.

Josephine looks over at me with a friendlier face. "But if you ever need any serious spell work done, you need to go see the spirit sisters."

"They're mediums and witches?"

"They're mediums. Their sister is a witch."

"Oh, good. Does she come for the festival and sell spell jars and voodoo dolls?"

There went the friendly face. What did I say?

"You really shouldn't make fun of things you don't understand, Ivy. It's not a good look, you know?"

"I didn't mean to make fun of anyone. It's just all so strange. Are you telling me the woman literally believes she's a witch?"

"A lot of people believe she's a witch."

"You believe in magic?"

"There's all sorts of magic. Everybody believes in some form of it, whether they want to acknowledge it or not."

Gran always talked about fairies as if they were real, and she definitely believed in things like meditating and manifesting, anything to do with the power of the mind. But I never thought of that stuff as magic. She was an artist. They're supposed to be quirky and free-spirited, right?

The sky turns dark on the drive back. "There's a thunderstorm coming," I say.

Josephine laughs. "That's snow, babe. There's a snowstorm coming."

"I forgot y'all get snow here. I'm used to all storms being thunderstorms. Unless they're tropical storms or hurricanes."

"That's terrifying. Maybe we'll get enough to do some snowshoeing."

"I don't have snowshoes. Should I have bought some?"

"Petra probably has a pair for you. She always knows what newbies need."

"What is she, like the fairy godmother of Ivydell?"

"Pretty much. I might not have survived my first year without her."

"I'm only going to be here for a few months. I can survive anything for that long."

Jensen is hunched under the open hood of a car when we drive back into Ivydell. Josephine reaches over and presses my horn. He looks up and waves.

She tells me to stop, and then she honks the horn again.

He shakes his head as he wipes his hands on a rag before he comes over.

"You rang?"

"It wasn't me."

"Her check engine light keeps coming on," she says.

"How long has that been happening?"

"I don't know." I chew my bottom lip. "A few weeks?"

"You drove all the way across the state with your check engine light on?"

"It wasn't constantly on. How do you know where I came

from?"

"Drive your car home and park it, beach bunny. I'll come by later and take a look at it."

"It's going to snow any minute," I say. "You need to put a shirt on."

"Any minute, huh?" He and Josephine exchange a look and both laugh.

I'm clearly not in on the joke because I have no idea what's so damn funny.

Jensen

Troubleshooting

OF COURSE, HER DAMN car is locked. I rap on her front door, probably also locked.

She opens the door like she's not expecting me. "Hi."

"I need your key."

"What?"

"To your car. So I can see why your check engine light keeps coming on?"

"Oh, yeah. Thanks for coming over to look at it."

"Don't thank me yet. You might not like what I find."

"What if there's really something wrong with it?"

"I'll fix it."

"What if you can't? Isn't there a lot of computerized stuff in newer cars? Did you go to school for that and get licensed or whatever?"

She's holding tight to her key like she's afraid to hand it over.

"You'll be happy to know I am actually a certified Ford mechanic."

"My car's a Toyota!"

"Are you trying to be funny right now?"

"Are you being willfully obtuse? There is a difference between a Ford and a Toyota."

"You're right. It's called a logo. Give me your key."

She finally gives it up. But she follows me outside.

"It runs okay?"

"It runs fine. No symptoms of anything being wrong other than the light intermittently coming on."

"Huh." I start the car and press the release for the gas cap, get out, and walk back to check the seal. "Your gas cap was loose. But if it's been happening for weeks, I have to assume you're intentionally not tightening it properly. Is there a reason for that?"

"You're not supposed to make it too tight."

"Please explain that theory."

"I read a story about a woman in Florida whose car exploded in a parking lot, and they said it happened because she had tightened her gas cap too much. They said you're supposed to leave it a little loose."

"Who's *they*?"

"Car experts, I guess. Maybe insurance investigators? Vehicles apparently catch on fire from it a lot."

"I know we just met, and you probably trust whatever website you read that shit on more than you do me, but I promise you *they* are wrong. Tighten the gas cap all the way."

"Are you sure?"

I hold the key out to her. "Positive."

"I'm going to Google it to double-check."

"I'd be shocked if you didn't."

"As soon as I can get the internet to work. I emailed Petra from my phone, but she hasn't responded yet. You don't happen to know how to get the Wi-Fi networks to show up, do you? Are they cloaked or something?"

"Cloaked?"

"For secrecy? I don't know."

"You have to plug into the phone line."

"The what?"

"Internet's still dial-up out here."

"That's outdated technology."

"Not in Ivydell."

"But that won't work."

"It works. It's just slow."

"I guess I can work on my phone until I get it figured out."

"Better work quick."

"What do you mean?"

"I hear it's going to snow any minute."

"What does snow have to do with anything?"

"Cell service gets spotty."

"Every time it snows?"

"And during heavy rains. Cloudy days."

"It has to be a bright, clear day for the internet to work?"

"As long as the phone lines aren't down."

"I need the internet to do my job. And I can only do so much on my phone. I have to use my computer for some stuff."

"Use your phone as a hotspot and get as much done as you can on your computer while you've still got cell service. That's not guaranteed out here either."

"Oh, yeah! That'll work. How'd you know that?"

"I wasn't raised in the wild."

"How long have you been here?"

"Four years."

"How old are you?"

"Twenty-nine. You?"

"Twenty-seven."

That's a little older than I would've guessed. I see her as less off-limits for a moment, but age has nothing to do with it. She's still too sweet for me. Too sweet to be here.

"How'd you hear about this place, Ivy?"

"It was my grandmother's favorite place in the world. And my mom lived here for the first thirteen years of her life."

"Interesting. I take it Ivydell was not your mom's favorite place."

"Can you fathom being a teenager here?"

"No. Your name makes sense now, though."

"If you say so." She laughs in the way people laugh at things they don't really find funny. "I can't imagine naming my kid after a place I hated. In her defense, she calls me Ivy, ignores the Dell. Only Gran ever called me by my full name."

"How long has she been gone?"

"Six months. How'd you know?"

"You talk about her in the past tense."

"Oh." She ducks her head, but I can see her lids blinking. "I didn't even realize I did that."

"It happens."

"What about you?" she asks, lifting her head enough for me to see her watery eyes. "How'd you find this place?"

"People who need Ivydell find it. Or someplace like it, I imagine."

She opens her mouth to say something else, but just smiles instead. And then, with no warning at all, she steps into my chest and hugs me. I know better than to hug her back. She doesn't belong in my arms.

But even I can tell when a woman needs to be held. Despite my better angels screaming all the reasons they shouldn't, my arms wrap around her. It's instantly too much warmth, too much tenderness—it's all too much.

And for the first time since I don't remember when, I don't want to let go.

Ivy

Catching Snowflakes

The last time a man cradled me against his naked chest, I knew a lot more about him than his name. And we weren't standing upright in my front yard with pillowy snowflakes being pierced by cactus thorns all around us like we'd been trapped in some sort of southwest-themed snow globe found at a truck stop, right next to a bag of beef jerky with a bible quote on it.

I pull back to end our hug and immediately miss the warmth of his skin. The solidness of him. His strength. "I'm sorry if I made things weird by hugging you."

"It's not weird." A large fluffy flake lands on his scorpion tattoo. For a fleeting few seconds before it melts, it appears to be balanced there like the tail's only purpose is to catch the best snowflakes and showcase them. "If you want, I can come in and light your fireplace for you before I go."

What I want most is to stay right where we are. I want the dome to remain sealed around us, sheltering us from everything beyond it. For the snow to fall just for us. For his body heat to melt it on contact. Contact. That's what I want.

It's too cloudy for a stunning sunset tonight, but I know it must be close to that time. The night will be dark, no stars visible.

The icy cold burns my cheeks. We have to go in. And eventually, he will have to go. But I do want the fire.

There is wood stacked in a rack next to my kiva fireplace. Behind the rack is a pile of newspapers. Jensen takes a sheet of the paper, twists it up like a torch and lights it. There are no logs in place yet, not even kindling. He reaches his hand up a few inches into the fireplace and lets the flame burn there.

"Why are you doing that?"

"I'm warming the chimney. Specifically, the air inside it. When it warms up, it gets lighter. That helps the air flow upward and keeps the smoke from backdrafting."

I wouldn't have known to do that.

He sets the newspaper down to finish burning and adds three logs to the fireplace, but he doesn't lay them flat. He positions each one slightly vertical with an end touching the back of the firebox, letting them cross over each other, but leaving plenty of open space between and around them.

"Why do you put the wood in that way?"

"These fireplaces are shallow. You can't build too big of a fire, and you have to leave room for air flow."

"Oh, okay. Thanks for showing me the proper technique."

He cuts a sharp look at me over his shoulder. I'm afraid at first that he might think I'm being a smartass, or making fun of the way he did it, but I really am grateful he showed me.

"I meant that sincerely."

"I know you did." He looks away just as quickly.

The room is suddenly shot through with tension. And something else. Vulnerability? For me, sure. But him? What is it for him? He might be a lot of things, but vulnerable doesn't make the list.

"You should let me repay you with dinner," I offer. "I'm making lasagna."

"Oh, yeah?"

"Yeah. I mean, it's frozen, but the picture on the box looks pretty tasty."

He laughs—with me, not at me. It's the first time I've been confident he wasn't mocking me. "Well, if you're going to go to all that trouble, I guess I could stay."

I marvel at the tone of his back muscles as he walks to the kitchen sink to wash his hands. "Do you need any help, or should I just get out of your way?"

"A team effort is always good. How about you open this bottle of wine while I turn on the oven and get glasses. Then you can pour while I put the lasagna in the oven."

"And then what?"

"Then we can enjoy the fire you built while we drink our wine and watch the snow fall on my patio."

"Hmm, so I lit the fireplace." He holds up one finger. "And now I'm going to open the wine. And then I'm going to pour the wine." Two more fingers go up. "But all you're going to do is put the food in the oven. It sounds like I'm doing most of the work here, which makes me wonder if that's a running theme with you. Are you always such a princess, Just Ivy?"

There is a challenge sparkling behind those sexy eyes of his, and I'm always up for a little flirty banter, especially when I can tell the other party believes he has me outgunned. Even more so when I think he might, too. I don't know quit, but I don't hate being taken down either.

"Sounds like you need to learn to count," I tease back. "I also got the glasses down, and I turned the oven on. Plus, I went to the store to buy the food and the wine. And I had to open the box the food came in. Who's really putting in the most effort here?"

The cork pops, and I feel it in my core.

"I guess I better do a better job of keeping up." He steps closer and hands me a glass of wine.

When I take the stem, I touch the rim of my glass to his. "Cheers to doing our share."

"How long does that lasagna have to cook?"

"Forty-five minutes." I take a sip of my wine.

"I bet I could even the score in half that time."

"Wow. I would've thought you'd be more competitive than that. But if you're willing to settle for a tie . . ."

"I didn't say I was going to roll over and take a nap the other half of the time."

My legs tremble, and he hasn't even touched me yet. I've been alone with a man before, but this feels like foreign territory. Like I've never been more out of my element.

I don't have a couch, just two small chairs and a bistro table—and my literally messy bed that I'm pretty sure is about to get metaphorically messy as well. No chance I'm sitting in one of those chairs. I sit on my bunched comforter, scoot back a few feet, and crisscross my legs, facing the glass door on the back wall.

Jensen takes a seat on the edge of the bed as well, but he doesn't move back. "If I'd known you wanted to buy wine, I would've told you about Hilltop. It's not much farther than the grocery store you went to, and they have a much better selection. Looks like any other convenience store, but they carry a lot of specialty stuff and good wines."

"You know a lot about wine?"

"I know a little." He grins, but doesn't say more.

I'm not sure if it's okay for me to ask what he means by that. How am I supposed to know where the boundaries lie? "Hilltop sounds like the Whole Foods of convenience stores."

"Pretty much."

"Whew, that fireplace gets warm quick. I'm going to take off my sweater. Just letting you know before I whip it off that I'm not stripping." Could my laugh be any more awkward? I swallow a gulp of wine before I reach to set it on the floor, nearly toppling over the edge of the bed to face-plant onto the Saltillo tile.

His grip is firm when he catches me and brings me back upright. When I'm steady on the mattress again, he takes my glass and sets it on the floor, placing his own right next to it.

He scoops me into the crook of his arm and pulls me onto his lap, straddling his thighs. His hands slide over my hips, under the hem of my sweater, brushing my skin and sparking a shiver of anticipation. He pushes the chunky cable-knit up a few inches before he closes his fists and continues to lift it, revealing my bare mid-drift as the tank top I'm wearing underneath slides up to the bottom of my ribs before it clings to me.

The sweater keeps going, and I lift my arms so he can pull it over my head. My hair gets tangled in it, but he carefully unwraps it without pulling at all. His rough fingers move gently over my skin, tracing the neckline of my thin tank and sending goosebumps down my arms.

I pull the tank off and shake my hair free. My nipples pebble under my sheer bra. His thumbs go straight to them, and the barely-there fabric between our skin prevents any friction, letting his fingers glide freely over and around them, dulling the sensation of his calloused skin abrading them. But I don't want anything dulled right now, so I reach back and unhook my bra.

Rounding my shoulders, I let the straps slide down my arms. The cups fall away, baring my breasts completely.

With one fluid movement, he flips us, pinning me under him and kissing me for the first time. This is so much better than the first kiss I was envisioning in the snow. Flames hiss in the fireplace and coyotes howl in the freezing nightfall while his tongue teases mine. I feel so completely protected. Sheltered.

His kiss trails down my neck to my chest. My back arches of its own accord when his mouth gets close to my nipple. It's a blatant display of need and I don't care. To say I've been in a dry spell for the past six months would be an understatement.

I haven't missed sex at all, but when his hot mouth closes over the stiff peak, my fingers sink into his hair, pulling him closer. He doesn't need the encouragement. And he damn sure doesn't need any direction.

A soft whimper leaves my mouth, becoming a desperate, mewling sound as he sucks harder. The feline contortions of my spine escalate as well. This is raw and feral and exactly the way I need it to be.

He shoves my leggings and panties down together. I bend my knees and toe the spandex and satin down my calves, kicking them off across the room. His hand massages my inner thigh as he moves it higher. When his fingers meet my smooth pussy, he moans, pulling his mouth off my nipple, leaving a cool sting that I instantly want him to soothe.

But he kisses his way down my torso. The scruff on his jaw

tickles my ribcage, making me squirm beneath him. The moment I wiggle, his erection surges against his zipper, pressing firmly into my leg. And my arousal becomes imminently obvious.

When he drops lower, his whiskers brush over my hipbone. I instinctively sink into the mattress to retreat. But when his shoulders slide between my legs and his thumbs spread my seam, he pauses there to watch my juices trickle from the opening that he's widened, and I'm stunned at the way I don't want to hide from this. The way I want to show him exactly how much he turns me on.

He presses two fingers inside me, and I moan as my walls clench. Looking down, I watch his eyes tracking his fingers as they slide slowly in and out of me. Watching him watch what he's doing to me is mesmerizing. I continue to watch as he extracts his fingers and sucks my essence off his skin. "I knew you were going to taste like regret."

"Regret?"

"Every time I see you, I'm going to want another taste. Having you around is going to make it impossible to think about anything else."

"But you still want me?"

"Want got left at the starting line five minutes after we met. I more than want you."

My body shudders as I watch his tongue replace his fingers. I let my head fall back onto the bed, knowing he might not be the only one who is going to regret this. But I couldn't care less right now because his hot mouth against my delicate skin is better than I imagined it would be—and I imagined it to be pretty damn good.

His head pivots from side to side as he eats me out like I've been presented to him on a platter. He's not afraid to make a mess, to explore my body like something urgent depends on it—and making me feel like it might.

The heightened sensation of his mouth on my clit, after he's been tongue-fucking me for longer than most men bother, nearly propels me straight up off the mattress. My high-pitched gasp only spurs him to fully ravage it with his tongue before lightly dragging his teeth over it, and then sucking it like he's read my goddamn instruction manual.

Like he wrote it.

My breath rushes out around strangled cries. He holds my legs open as they strain to close and sucks the final orgasmic shrieks from my body, licking up my sweet release before he frees his hard cock.

I assume he'll want that oral session repaid, but he doesn't even hint at bringing his erection to my mouth. He makes quick work of dispatching his jeans and underwear, and then he nudges my legs farther apart with his knee. Not that it takes much effort. I have all the strength of cooked spaghetti. With a firm grasp on my hips, he pulls me lower, positioning me exactly where he wants me. My hair fans out behind me as I slide down.

His body covers mine as he lowers his face to kiss me. I taste myself on his tongue but don't pull away. When he realizes I'm going to kiss him back so completely, he groans into my mouth.

The twitch of his dick between my legs causes my walls to clench.

He palms my drenched pussy and closes his eyes for a few moments. They're hooded when he opens them and stares at me. "This sweet little snatch is so swollen. Why? What does it need?"

"Your thick cock filling it, stretching me—"

I don't get another syllable out before he's granting my wish.

He doesn't worry about lining up the tip at my entrance first, doesn't proceed a few inches and wait for my response, but he isn't rough and uncaring, just hard and hungry. I draw a deep breath when he enters me, and hold it until he's fully seated. His entire length invades my body without hesitation, going all the way to the hilt in one smooth stroke.

I feel every bit of the stretch his thickness demands, the total fullness of him inside me. There is a light sheen of sweat already forming at the nape of his neck when my fingers thread into his hair. My exhale brings a hint of relaxation to my muscles, but it's short-lived.

His strokes are long and forceful and my walls clamp involuntarily, desperate to hold him inside, and then welcome him back every time. He fucks me like this isn't our first time, like there is no reason for caution, not a chance I won't want exactly what he wants—or would deny him, regardless. His confidence in his skills is overt and sexy as hell.

I've never enjoyed being treated like I might break in bed. I want to be used, not wasted.

And he is using me so well. His hips pull again, and my eyelids flutter as he presses against a sensitive spot that I'm sure has a corresponding letter, but I never remember which one is G or A or whatever else has been discovered because there is no internal spot that gets me off. But that doesn't mean it doesn't feel incredible to have it stroked just right.

An even better feeling is when Jensen's body tenses, and I know the stroke feels so right for him, too. He looks away as if making eye contact would ruin it. I'm not offended. I understand it.

We can't keep things entirely dispassionate because there is an undeniable connection, but we don't have to embellish it. The base enjoyment of each other's bodies can be enough.

My eyes close, and I rock my hips up to meet his next thrust, determined to enjoy the pressure as long as he can provide it.

I'm panting and barely able to speak, but I need him to know I'm okay with him keeping some emotional distance. "Fuck me like you don't know my name. Or the color of my eyes. Or that I drove all the way across the state with my gas cap intentionally loosened."

I open my eyes to see his smile struggling to break through a grimace as his muscles all seize, and his body convulses through his orgasm. When it subsides, he collapses on me and laughs freely.

His voice is brusque and steamy in my ear. "Your name is Ivy Dell McAdams. Your eyes are hazel. You have no business operating a motor vehicle . . . and I wish you'd never come here."

The oven timer dings. "No, you don't. If I'd never come here, you wouldn't be having lasagna for dinner tonight."

There is still a half-frozen island in the middle of the pan. The oven thermostat apparently can't be trusted. We eat around the edges and finish my cheap bottle of wine.

It's barely snowing when he leaves, but I make him wear a t-shirt that belonged to an ex. I've had the shirt longer than I had the guy, so I'm not sacrificing a special memento. Jensen rolls his eyes at my insistence, but he pulls it over his head anyway.

He kisses me softly, and he doesn't look away when he says goodnight.

Jensen

Fuel to the Fire

SOMETIMES YOU'RE RUNNING AWAY; sometimes, you're just gone for a while. In Ivydell, we're free to come and go like the wind—no ties to bind. At least, that's how it's supposed to be.

I only left for two days, but when I step out of the bathroom, freshly showered and barely covered, Petra is waiting for me at my kitchen table like a bounty hunter who's tracked down her skip. She warms her hands around a mug of coffee with a triumphant expression, knowing she took me by surprise. I jump like a goddamn jackrabbit when I see her.

"Jesus! You scared the shit out of me. Knock. Knock." I clutch the towel at my waist to keep it secure, thankful I bothered with one. She's lucky it's colder than a witch's tit in a brass bra outside or she'd be watching my dick bounce. Not that she'd give a shit about seeing it.

"I knocked. You didn't hear me."

"What are you doing here?"

"You don't bother to let anybody know when you take off for days on end?"

"Cujo knew. Why does it matter?"

"People depend on you around here. The least you could do is—"

"No, fuck that. That's not the deal. I'm not obligated to do any of the stuff I do around here."

"Fair enough, but if you don't want people to rely on you anymore, you need to man up and say so. Give them a heads up before you bail."

"I'm not leaving. And I didn't say I didn't want to help anybody anymore. I've been gone for longer than a few days before, and it's never been a problem. What's really going on, Petra?"

Her nostrils flare. I feel mine do the same. A pissing contest between two equally stubborn people won't accomplish a damn thing. Yet here we are, staring at each other like neither wants to be the first to break, except I don't even know what I'm defending. I honestly don't have the first clue what she's pissed off about.

Petra and I have never had a problem. She's the queen bee around here, and I'm the first one to say she deserves the title.

"Look, whatever I've done, it was unintentional, okay?"

"Pfft."

Damn, I'd rather be punched in the mouth than see that look of disgust in her eyes.

"What did I do? Just say it!"

"Stay away from Ivy."

Whoa. Didn't see that coming. "You're policing my personal life now?"

"Oh, don't act like I'm trying to turn you into a monk. You can take your rugged good looks and devil-may-care attitude into any bar you want and let women throw pussy at you like beads at Mardi Gras whenever you feel the need, but leave her alone, Stinger."

"Why?"

She looks away, stares at my fireplace like there's a movie playing in it. Her eyes track something mine don't see.

"Her grandmother was very special to me."

"And you promised her on her deathbed you'd watch out for her granddaughter? Is that why she's here?"

"No. But it doesn't matter because I'm going to watch out for her, anyway."

"Ivy's an adult. She's twenty-seven-years-old."

"I don't care if she's fifty-seven-fucking-years-old! She's emotionally fragile right now. The last thing she needs is a man like you in her life."

"What does that mean, a man like me?" I know exactly what it means, but I'd like to think I'm wrong, to believe she thinks better of me than that. Truth be told, my plan when I left was to occupy myself with someone new for a few days to get Ivy out of my head, so yeah, maybe I am a man like that. But it wasn't enough time to find a woman I wanted to look twice at.

"I have no intentions of doing anything to hurt, Ivy."

But I've got a bad feeling she could leave me staring into fireplaces for the rest of my life if I'm not careful.

"Your good intentions aren't enough."

"I can't tell you what you want to hear. I don't make false promises. You know so much about me, I'd think you'd know that."

"No matter what you intend in the moment, please don't make her any promises at all, Stinger. Can you at least give me that?"

I nod. "No promises."

She narrows her eyes at me like she's unsure if I meant I guaranteed I wouldn't make Ivy any promises or confirmed that I couldn't guarantee it. Honestly, I'm not sure myself, but if I do make her any promises, I'll keep them. There's no question about that.

There are five rapid knocks on my door. I already know it's Ivy. She's impatient by nature, and it's freezing out there. I'm not expecting her, but I wasn't expecting my current guest either.

When I open the door, she's bouncing on her toes and rubbing her hands together. Her hair is in a ponytail and her cheeks are flushed. She's wearing a sweater that doesn't stand a chance at deflecting the wind.

"Do you not own a coat?"

"Do you not own clothes?"

Shit. I forgot I was still wearing nothing but a towel. "Come inside."

She smiles when she sees Petra. "Oh, good. Josephine said she thought you might be here. Are you still up for hanging out this afternoon? I'm really looking forward to talking to you."

"Yeah, hon. Sure."

Petra stands like she's ready to go, but I heard the hesitation in her voice. She sets her coffee cup in the sink, and her shoulders tense before she turns back around. "I just need to take care of a few things first. I'll come by your place in about an hour. Is that good?"

Ivy looks wary. "Yeah, that's fine. I'll be there."

As soon as Petra leaves, Ivy throws up her hands. "She keeps putting me off, even when she makes the plans. Am I that horrible to be around?"

So much for not wanting promises made to Ivy to be broken. Maybe Petra should hold herself to the same standard.

"You are not at all horrible to be around. Petra likes to be in control. I understand she and your grandmother were close. It's probably just hard for her, knowing she might get emotional talking about her."

"But you can't just bottle it up and refuse to face it. That only makes things worse. I'm trying to be patient, but I uprooted my whole life to come here. She said she would tell me things, but so far all she's done is avoid me. It's getting hard not to be pissed off about it. If I'd known she didn't want me here, I wouldn't have bothered."

"It's not that she doesn't want you here, Ivy." I take a step toward her, and my towel falls to the floor. Before I can bend to retrieve it, she stomps on the edge.

"Leave it," she says. "My knees need it more than you do." She lowers to the floor in front of me, and her pouty smile when she looks up at me is devastatingly beautiful. "I have a little time to kill before I get my hopes crushed again."

I know the thin towel is no cushion against the tile floor, but she swirls the tip of her tongue along the underside of my hard-on from root to tip like she's perfectly comfortable there. There is nothing outside the walls of Ivydell that compares to this. She flattens her tongue to massage the swollen vein she's just traced. Her warm, soft mouth cradles me all the way down, causing me to twitch and shudder. When she reaches the base, she moves lower to suck on my tight balls, and it's all I can do not to fist her ponytail and pull her face up enough to shove my dick between her lips. But I want her to take her time as much as I want to feel my cock in her throat.

When she licks the pre-cum off the head, my eyes close and my lungs evacuate their deepest recesses. I inhale as her saliva spills down my length and open my eyes to watch her take me to the back of her throat.

My breath is already erratic when she hollows her cheeks and makes an erotic show of pulling off slowly before sliding her mouth back down, twisting her head from side to side.

I can't hold off pushing my fingers into her hair any longer, spreading them under her ponytail to hold her head. She bobs her head, taking her pacing cue from the pressure of my palm. Fuck, she's good.

Looking down at her, I know I wouldn't do a thing in this world to hurt her, but if she asked me to promise her the moon right now, I might do it.

She looks up at me, and the sight of her watering eyes lights a fuse in my core. My ass clenches and my dick surges, and when I explode, it feels like salvation. But I know in the seconds that follow what it really is: annihilation. Obliteration of walls I built to last.

Petra's right. I should stay away from this woman. But I told her the truth when I said I can't. It's too soon for the pull to be this strong, but it's not like I'm in control here.

The only option I see is to let the flame burn hot and fast for the next few months and hope it chokes itself out. Seems like the most likely outcome, and we're both adults. We can handle it.

Petra

Promises Kept

My fingertips trace the swirls on the canvas. Patrice's fine brush strokes under my dry skin, her muted desert tones under my inflamed cuticle . . . she was always softer, more refined. It's the only one of her paintings I have. She knew how much I loved this one, so she snuck it into my car, even though I was being a stubborn ass and refusing to speak to her on our last day.

We were all packed up. I wanted to stay and make the bastards drag me away, but I wasn't entirely selfish. If we stood a chance at beating them in court, we all had to go peacefully. I couldn't jeopardize everyone else's chances for the sake of my ego.

Funny how I could see that so clearly, but couldn't tell what my ego was doing in other areas of my life. I knew she had to start over, take her daughter somewhere she could have a normal life. But I really thought she'd come back when we won.

It was such a long battle, but it was never hers. Now she's gone.

And it's not her daughter who's come with questions; it's her granddaughter, who is the spitting image of Patrice. Aside from the red hair, Ivy looks just like her. Same smile. Same eyes. Same tenacity.

I smile as I go over the angel in the storm clouds. She's too much like her grandmother to let me off the hook. I promised her answers. It's time to make good on it.

Be with me, Patty.

Ivy

Lightning Round

I GO OVER THE list of questions I've prepared for Petra. The list is ridiculously long, and I can't hit her with all of them today, but there is so much I want to know. Do I start small and build to the biggest one? What if she won't sit down with me again? I've been here almost a week already.

And I've already seen Jensen's dick twice. I guess it's true what they say. The desert changes people.

The woman I was last week wouldn't have believed this development. Not that I was a prude back then, but I probably would've at least waited until I'd seen him with a shirt on. On the other hand, given that he's been half naked since we met, it's a wonder I've only seen it twice.

I don't regret either session, but it's weird how he doesn't feel like a stranger. He should feel more like a one-night stand than a friend with benefits. It's not the fact that I've seen his dick twice that feels the most shocking; it's the fact that I'm so confident I'll be seeing it again soon. Cocksure. Can women be cocksure? Because I'm pretty sure about his cock. Far less sure about the rest of him.

My phone buzzes. I assume it's Mom, checking in for the third time today. She isn't as subtle as she thinks. It's obvious she doesn't believe I'll last the entire two months, but I will. She'll see. Plus, she's worried. I get that, but it's not like I'm going to get eaten by a bear. The fiercest wildlife I've seen is a badger, and I was inside, so it wasn't an in-the-wild encounter.

Granted, it scared the piss out of me because it was nearly dark out and it waddled right up to my back patio, but when I shrieked from the safe side of the glass door, it went back the way it came. Josephine said I probably wouldn't see another one for a while because they don't come around much until spring. She sprayed some citronella oil around my patio and said it would keep them away, but I think that was mostly for my peace of mind.

That ominous striped face in the dusk will never leave my mind, but it hasn't come back to my patio. Yet.

Mom's excuses for reaching out continue to amuse me, though. So far today, she's let me know she ran into my eighth-grade boyfriend in the grocery store and we're getting a late red tide at home. The algae bloom wreaks havoc on my allergies, so when I'm there, knowing it's coming is useful information, but since I'm nine hours away, I can breathe easy. Dust is my biggest nemesis here.

I look at my screen to see what breaking news alert she's come up with now. This message isn't from Mom; it's from my coworker, Zara.

> **WHERE THE HELL ARE YOU?**

> I'm in west Texas. Way, way west Texas.

Why?

Long story. It's only for a few months.

Are you okay? Your last post looks like you're being held in a refugee camp.

Offensive on so many levels. The desert is supposed to look desolate in February.

Stay in touch!

Okay, but I promise I'm fine.

Petra's gentle knock causes me to jump.

I know it's not Jensen because his knock is harder and more spaced out—like someone using a giant forged doorknocker in a castle. *Dear God, he's knocked on my door once and I think I know his knock. I seriously need to stop.*

And it can't be Josephine because she just slaps the door once and yells, "It's me!" before she tries the knob to see if it's locked. It's always locked. Locking the front door is a habit I can't break, not that I plan to try.

"You actually made it."

"I deserved that." Petra tucks her head as she steps inside.

"Sorry. I didn't mean it to come out that way. I'm just really glad you came."

She holds up a couple of photo albums. "Thought you might like to look through these."

"Yeah. As long as we can talk about them while we look." I'm not trying to be confrontational, but if she thinks I'll get distracted with some old pictures and that'll be all it takes to satisfy my curiosity, she needs to know she's wrong.

She sets them on my table. "Happy to talk about them. You mind if we raise a toast to the occasion? Patrice would say she needed a shot to warm her bones in February." She pulls a brown bottle from a saddle blanket tote that looks like she's had it since the last time she drank with Gran. "Though if we're being honest, she was always more of a sipper than a shooter."

"I've been known to sip a little ski." I bring glasses to the table with a smile. "Shoot it on occasion."

"I guess you've been told your whole life how much you look like her."

"A few times. She always told me not to listen, that I was a beauty, but I loved hearing it because she was beautiful to me."

"She was absolutely beautiful." Petra pours a few inches of the amber liquid for each of us and lifts her glass. "To Patty."

I freeze, with my glass halfway to hers. "I never heard anyone call her that before. Did she know you called her Patty?"

When our glasses meet, she nods. "She knew."

She takes a sip of her whiskey, but I throw mine back in one go. "In the letter I found, you wrote Patrice, not Patty."

"Felt like maybe I shouldn't call her that anymore. I never asked if someone new was calling her Patty. Guess I wasn't ready to know. Didn't want it to matter." She takes another sip. "I wasn't too good at dealing with things I didn't want to face back then. Holding on to the past was easier. It felt right to imagine she'd come back, and we'd pick up where we left off."

"I am such a fucking idiot. All this time . . . I honestly didn't know. It seems so obvious now, but—"

"There was no reason you should've known."

"She never moved on with anyone new."

"I know. Your mom sent me a letter. I called just in time to talk to her before she got too bad to speak. She was weak, but I'm grateful to your mom for reaching out. It meant the world to hear Patty's voice one last time."

"You must've been like a second mom to my mom when she was growing up out here."

"No. Patty was an amazing mom, but I wasn't good with kids. I loved CiCi because she was a part of Patty, but I never got to know her like I should have. Probably made her feel like she was in the way more often than not. She wasn't, but I didn't know how to interact with her, so I held her at arms-length. It wasn't intentional."

"You give everyone nicknames, don't you? Nobody calls my mom CiCi. She's Cecilia."

"Cecilia Cathleen. I remember. If it weren't for me, Patty would've moved her away from here a lot sooner. I was selfish. It's a wonder your mom doesn't hate me."

"She hates this place, but she's never said a bad word about you."

"She probably wouldn't have in front of Patty. She loved her mom."

"So did you." It's strange to hear Gran called Patty, but I like that Petra is using that name for her in front of me now. Makes me feel like less of a bother, more like someone she actually wants to share stories about Gran with.

"I did. So much." She pours more whiskey and opens the top photo album.

Some images I've seen before, but I'm amazed at how many I haven't. I stare at a picture of my mom toddling toward a prairie dog up on its haunches, wary of the chubby little girl who appears to be squealing with delight, laughing like she thinks they can be playmates. She was happy then, still too little to want for anything outside of Ivydell. CiCi, before she had a care in the world.

We spend hours making our way through birthday pictures and photos of the Ivydell Festival in its early years. She has pictures from when Ivydell was originally settled, which was before her time here. Petra tells me stories to narrate the pictorial history. So few modern conveniences, long before the lack of Wi-Fi, but so much determination in their eyes.

And a shit ton of indifference to mainstream society, long before the counterculture and free love movement of the sixties. This places dates back further than I knew.

"Looks like a livelier place back then."

"It was."

"Why do you think Gran didn't come back when you wrote to her?"

"She was already where she wanted to be, with you and your mom."

"Mom says that, too. But I think there's more to it. Her paintings from the desert are different. They always seemed more expressive to me. I think she deeply missed it. The beach never spoke to her in the same way."

"You can miss one place while loving another. She loved the beach."

"She grew to love it, but this was her first love." I think Petra was her first love, too, but I don't feel like I have a right to speak my opinion on that.

"Sometimes, we want to make things more complicated than they are. She didn't come back because she was happy where she was."

"Maybe."

The pictures of my mom change from a happy little girl to a sullen preteen. I never think of my mom as angry, but she is full of resentment in these pictures, more than the average kid. It doesn't look like she ever smiled past the age of maybe ten or eleven. Thank goodness she got out at thirteen. I know it was hard to adjust, but I can't imagine how hard it would've been for her to live anywhere else if she'd stayed here until she was grown and could leave on her own.

Her stories all carry more weight now that I'm here and looking into her face when she was here.

"She looks sour," Petra says. "And she was a lot of the time, but she loved the festival. It was a link to the outside. She got to see kids who went to regular schools and had friends their own age. I knew she deserved a life like that. Patty knew, too."

"But she didn't leave until she had to, until everyone had to go."

"She was leaving, anyway."

"What?"

"She'd already made plans to leave before we got the news. I asked her to stay until the end, three months longer than she'd intended. We fought most of it. The tension was constant. It wasn't fair to her, and it damn sure wasn't fair to your mom. I should've accepted her decision when she made it, instead of prolonging the inevitable."

"Why didn't you leave with her?"

"It's complicated."

"Is it really? Or do you just not want to face the simplicity of the truth?"

"Oh, you are definitely Patty's granddaughter." She shakes her head as she closes the album. "I'll leave these with you for a while. You can go through the rest on your own. If you have questions, let me know."

"I think I'm going to be stuck on my last question."

"You'll get unstuck. We all do, eventually." She pauses at my door and turns around to face me again. "Hey, Ivy?"

"Yeah?

"Stay away from Stinger."

"Why?"

"I don't want you to get hurt."

"How do you know I won't hurt him?"

"I don't. But I already asked him to stay away from you."

"What did he say?"

"He said no promises."

"I gotta say the same. And I think if Gran was here, she'd tell me to trust my gut."

"No doubt she would. Goodnight, Ivy Dell."

"Night." I don't correct her. She can use my middle name. I'm a link to Patty for her, just like she's a link to Gran for me. Missing links.

I've sure missed a hell of a lot.

Jensen

Cat on a Cold Dirt Road

I PULL ALONGSIDE IVY, casually strolling down the road like she's unaware she could be in danger. To be fair, she doesn't know about the sighting, but she's not paying attention to her surroundings at all. She's not at the beach anymore. Although, that's another place she should probably pay attention to what's happening around her. It's a wonder she didn't get swept out to sea before she made it to adulthood.

"Get your phone out of your face and get in the truck."

"Hi. I'm good. How are you?"

"Get in the truck, Ivy."

"Are pictures not allowed here? Didn't know I was breaking any law."

"You looking to get an up close and personal shot of a mountain lion?"

"I can see for miles in every direction. No big cats."

"They're stalker predators. By the time you see them, you're in trouble. Get in this truck before I get out and physically force you into it."

She looks alarmed. By my threat or the possibility of a mountain lion, I'm not sure, but at least she's paying attention now. "Is there really a mountain lion in Ivydell?"

"Unless you doubt Petra's ability to recognize one, yes."

Her feet move quick when she's motivated. The slamming of my truck door has never sounded better. She's safely inside and that's all that matters.

"It's good to see you actually own a coat."

"Are mountain lions frequent visitors?"

"No. Their prey won't usually try to cross the cattle guard to come inside. And mountain lions rarely follow roads out in the open. They prefer to stay hidden. You'll occasionally see one crossing the main road on the way in, but they don't walk along it in plain sight. It'd be unusual for one to walk through the gate."

"They can't jump the fence?"

"It's unlikely. The fence is twelve-feet high. They can't usually jump higher than ten. And the wire is nearly impossible for them to climb."

"Nearly. That's not very reassuring. Where are we going?"

"To Cujo's."

"Why?"

"He's better equipped to handle this."

"I don't want to know what that means."

"Petra scared it. She said it headed back up front. Hopefully, it kept going until it was outside again."

"How would we know?"

"There are trail cams that monitor the gate on both sides. I'll look at the footage, but I want to let Cujo know as soon as possible, and he's not answering his phone."

"You couldn't have just texted him?"

"Not sure when he'd see it if he's not answering his phone. Sometimes, he turns it off."

"That doesn't seem wise, living out here."

"His business if he wants his phone on or not."

"Right."

I tell her to wait in the truck when we get to Cujo's. The door opens before I knock. He rubs his hand over his face, says he was asleep, but he heard my truck pull up. After I've given him the update, he walks to the truck with me, veering to the passenger side as I slide behind the wheel.

Ivy rolls down her window, and he offers his huge mitt. Her hand looks tiny in his. They introduce themselves.

He smiles at me and shakes his head before he walks away. I don't need him to tell me what he's thinking. I guess everybody's got thoughts about Ivy and me. They can all fuck off and mind their own damn business.

"He looks scary," Ivy says as I drive off.

"I'm sure under the right circumstances, he could be."

"Are you scared of him?"

"Haven't had a reason to be so far."

"Are there any quirky but not shady people who live out here?"

"Josephine comes to mind."

"True. She and I went shopping together. Speaking of shopping, we should go to Hilltop and check out that wine selection you told me about."

"You and Josephine?"

"I meant you and me."

"You busy right now?"

"Not unless you count hiding from a mountain lion."

I stop at the shop on the way out and let her watch the trail cam footage with me, holding my breath and hoping to see that cat walk out the same way it came in. And there it is, tail dragging the ground on its way out.

"Wow. I've never seen one this close before." Her eyes stretch wide.

"I had to have been out in the bay when it walked past. Never saw it."

Guess I can stop judging her for not being observant enough. How the hell was I out there, moving shit around and that cat just strolled on by with neither of us taking notice of the other? It may have seen me, but I was fucking oblivious. It's good to have a guardian angel.

The relief on Ivy's face softens her features. She's got her own angelic qualities.

"Let's go buy some wine."

Ivy

Bitter Notes

OUR QUEST MAY HAVE originally been for wine, but Hilltop's chocolate section has me in a trance. I've been regretting not bringing any with me to Ivydell. That clearance Valentine's Day candy was great for road snacks, but it's lost its appeal.

Jensen backtracks to find me when he realizes I'm no longer following him. "I thought we were here for wine."

"We are. But chocolate." I'm practically salivating. "Look at all of it."

He grabs four bars and a bag of truffles. "Come with me."

I trail him to the wine, but not without protest. "I don't even know what you picked out. What if I don't like any of it?"

"If you don't like my choices, you don't deserve chocolate."

"Oh, excuse me, Willy Wonka. I didn't realize you were an expert."

"You should trust me. I have excellent taste." He spins to face me with a mischievous grin on his face and pins me against an end-cap of fancy crackers before I have time to react. "In wine, women, and chocolate."

His kiss is too passionate for public display—and too good to resist.

Looking into his eyes when he backs up and gives me room to

breathe again, I return the playful smile. I swear it's like he knows just how much I'll let him get away with. From what I hear, he wouldn't be the only psychic around. He makes me wish I was one. I'd love to know what brought him to Ivydell.

A man's voice calls out to him. "Stinger! I was hoping you'd show up soon. I've got something for you."

"Stop scaring me, Shane. Your enthusiasm makes me think I'm about to spend too much money in here."

"There's no such thing as spending too much money on wine."

We turn down the aisle where the man is holding up a bottle.

They slip effortlessly into a language I don't understand, using words like biodynamic, brix, and terroir. That last word I sort of understand, but only because I have friends who love day trips to wineries. I love them, too, but I tag along for the tasting, not to learn anything.

I listen to them carry on, talking about wine like mad scientists, and it becomes clear Jensen doesn't just know one type of wine from another; he understands wine making in intricate detail. I'm a wine enthusiast in that I get enthused about drinking it. He's something else. Something unexpected, to say the least.

Shane doesn't have to twist Jensen's arm to get him to take two bottles of the wine they've been discussing. He walks us up to the register. "I can't wait to hear what you think."

"You know I'll tell you," Jensen says.

"And you know I value your opinion. Enjoy." They shake hands, and Shane goes back to stocking his wine shelves.

Jensen tells the cashier we'll take two of the Caprese sandwiches, a pint of pesto pasta salad, and some of the mixed olives from the display case.

"Do you have time for a picnic?"

"Sure." I thought people only went on picnics in movies. He needs to slow down on the surprises. I'm too young for a heart attack. And I still don't know how far we are from a hospital.

He asks the cashier if they have any plastic wine glasses.

She tells him they have stemless ones, pointing to the row lined up along the top of the food case. I think he meant disposable glasses, but these are reusable and have the market's logo printed on them.

"I never noticed those. Are they new?"

"Just got them in. You'll be the first customer to buy one."

"I'll take two."

The snow that fell during our first kiss has been long melted, and no flakes have fallen since, but I feel the same warm flutters in my stomach as he drives us back in the direction of Ivydell. He turns off on a different dirt road, though. This one isn't far from Hilltop, so it's at a higher elevation, which doesn't seem to make much of a difference until Jensen takes a cut-off that leads to a dead end with a view that stretches forever. He backs in and lowers the tailgate.

Sunrise was hours ago and sunset is still twice as many hours away, but we don't need either of those things to make this panorama worth it. The desert looks completely flat from some vantage points, but from here, we can see the gentle roll of the plains. It's cold, but peaceful. The brutal wind that blew yesterday has given us a break today.

Jensen wrestles his keys from his pocket and flips open a corkscrew.

I laugh. "You have a corkscrew on your keychain?"

"You don't?"

"Seriously, what's your background with wine?"

"I grew up in wine country."

"Feels like your knowledge is a little more fine-tuned than that."

"Yeah, okay. My family owned a winery. It was founded by my grandfather. Dad grew up working it and ultimately inherited it."

"You grew up working it, too, right?" I unwrap sandwiches while he opens the wine.

"I did. And then I inherited it. And then I sold it."

"Don't want to carry on the family tradition?"

"If I ever make wine, it won't be according to family tradition."

He hands me a glass. I want to ask so many more questions, but if he wants to say more, he will.

We finish our sandwiches and take turns passing the pasta salad between us, eating off the same plastic fork. I pick an olive from the container with my hand and press it to his lips. He pretends he's going to bite my fingers. I yank them away out of instinct, but he guides my hand back to his mouth, taking just the olive with his teeth, and then kissing my fingers.

I hold my wine up to see how the sunlight shines through it. It's a dark red, but it's got a mellow flavor. "It's a pretty color. And it tastes good. That's the extent of my wine knowledge."

He rolls his glass until the wine sloshes up to the rim. "Nice purple hue. You can pick up some blue when it thins against the light. Low acidity. Dark fruit. There's nothing wrong with appreciating a wine for its color and taste."

"Your appreciation is a lot more in depth than mine."

"The consumer liking the end product matters more than their ability to dissect it."

"True." I take another drink of the wine.

We sit quietly for a while, but it's not uncomfortable. It's an easy silence until I break it. "Such a pretty day."

"Yeah." He pushes the cork back into the wine. "It's a good day to take advantage of the internet being stable. I assume you're probably supposed to be working."

He's ending our picnic so abruptly I'm at a loss for words. I nod and finish my wine. What made him switch from enjoying my company to being eager to take me home?

"It's not as unreliable as you said. I was logged on for nine hours a few days ago, and I was on for about four hours yesterday, even with all the wind."

"You enjoyed that way too much."

"Working?"

"Telling me I was wrong." He smiles, but there's something missing from it now.

"For what it's worth, you were right about it being slow."

When we turn onto the dirt road that leads to Ivydell, the whole world looks flat again. The mesa sits unchanged, clearly present but seemingly unreachable.

Jensen slows to a stop in front of my casita. "Don't forget your chocolate."

I take it all without opening the bag to look through it, not asking if he wants any of it.

Inside, I power up my laptop and dump the bag out onto my table, grabbing a bar indiscriminately. The label says Bitter Dark. Of course, he'd choose that.

Jensen

Comfortably Numb

I'M SURE IVY THINKS I'm an asshole after the way I ran hot and cold on her the other day, but I did her a favor. She was about to ask questions I didn't want to answer. It was my own damn fault for opening up about the winery. She's too easy to talk to. Five minutes in her presence and I can feel my guard melting around the edges like butter in a hot pan.

There's almost always something to keep my hands busy around here, but not this weekend. Nobody's having car trouble, no holes in the fence that need to be repaired, no projects to be built for anyone. Normally, I make the most of my downtime. It's when I hike, fish, or get in the truck and drive until something catches my eye, explore. But when I think about doing those things today, my next thought is to invite Ivy.

She probably wouldn't go, anyway, but I probably wouldn't enjoy it without her either.

And if I'm being honest, I still want to know what she's doing here. I know she wanted to see this place because of her grandmother, but I think she has other reasons, too. Grief is a bitch, but that's not the only thing driving her. Maybe none of us is driven by a singular horror.

I hear Cujo's pipes before I see the cloud of dust he's riding in on. He pulls up into the bay out of the wind, jams his kickstand down, and steps off his bike, looking like a leather-clad giant. "What are you doing today?"

"Haven't decided yet." I toss some bolts into a box. Cleaning up and organizing parts keeps my hands busy, but the rest of me is still restless.

"I keep telling you I can get you a good deal. You'd always have something to do if you had a bike."

"Work on it?"

He laughs. "That, too. But it'd be nice to have somebody out here to ride with."

We'd make a hell of an odd pair riding together, him with his patches and me without. I like the guy, but I'm not sure I want to ride next to him. Don't want to draw any false associations. Or get caught in any crossfire. I'm told he's more of an auxiliary member of the motorcycle club that's represented on his jacket, but I've never been clear on exactly what that means. And I damn sure know better than to ask for clarification.

He rolls a bolt between his thumb and index finger before he tosses it into the box. "Feel like fishing?"

"In this wind? Sounds like a waste of gas and bait." It's over an hour's drive to get to the nearest water worth fishing.

"Probably. Can't help but notice you've been around a lot lately. Doesn't seem like you're getting out much."

"I'm okay." With his rough exterior, Cujo looks like the last guy who'd be able to tell when somebody is in a dark place, but he's good at reading people. He cares.

"Quit moping around out here. Go let that new redhead suck your dick."

I said he cares, not that he has any couth about him. "I doubt she's got any interest in doing that."

He mounts his bike, rights it between his legs, and walks it backwards out of the bay. "Maybe you should try to convince her. Make it your fucking mission, man. You need one."

When he starts it up, the rumbling beneath my feet feels like the tremors in the ground I grew up with. It's weird the things you miss sometimes. An earthquake will get your blood pumping. It's not lost on me that's the thing I actually miss—the adrenaline.

Cujo rides off and the ground calms.

I always figured when I got bored in Ivydell, that would be my sign to leave. The calm was what I was seeking. The nothingness of it all. Not feeling anything and not being expected to. I told myself when the numb wore off, I'd move on. But I'm not ready to go.

Why'd she have to come here and remind me what it was like to feel more? Crave more.

Fuck. I know it's not fair to blame her. She's pretty and interesting; it's only natural to feel a little excited about her, even when she's not with me. I'm projecting shit onto her that's not hers to bear.

Hell, what I'm feeling could've been spiked by that mountain lion wandering through. I don't want it to come back, but it got my blood pumping. Mountain lions, earthquakes . . . maybe I'm just naturally attracted to situations where my odds are bad.

Ivy's not a mission, regardless. She feels more like a respite, but she's here to hide from her own shit, not to shield me from mine.

Ivy

Definitely Not a Soccer Mom

I CAN'T REMEMBER THE last time I slept this late. I'm afraid to look at my emails. While coffee's brewing, I tether my phone to my computer and try to log on. I've got no signal. No bars, no hope. Shit. This is bad. I'm supposed to be online for a meeting in thirty minutes. Maybe by the time I get out of the shower, I'll be able to connect.

My bathroom smells amazing as soon as I lather my hair. A few drops of Petra's peppermint oil in my shampoo was definitely a good idea. I've got plenty left for my car when the chipmunks come back. The lavender oil I added to my conditioner has me taking deep inhales, too. Josephine gives good tips.

Still not sure about the risks she's willing to take where men are concerned, but hey, whatever arrangement she and Cujo are good with is none of my business.

The whole casita smells like fresh-cut herbs as I walk back to the computer, towel-drying my hair. Still no signal. I'll be lucky if I don't get fired before my lease here is up.

That thought would make some people consider leaving early. It makes me want to stay longer.

I raise the blinds on the small window in my kitchen, but I can only see to the edge of the road. A curtain of blowing dust blocks my view beyond that. Pouring my coffee, I contemplate crawling back into bed. May as well. I'm for sure missing that meeting.

What a clusterfuck of a day, and it's not even noon.

I send Mom a text to let her know I'm alive and to say I love you. There's never much to tell her, which I'm sure makes her think I'm hiding something. But the velocity of the wind and the stability of the internet are about the biggest changes to be expected from one day to the next.

Aside from the excitement of the mountain lion visitor. And my time with Jensen. I may never tell her about either of those. I'm honestly not sure which one would concern her more.

I sit at the table and look through the photo albums Petra left while I sip my coffee. The pictures of her and Gran look different now. How could I never have realized they were a couple? It's so obvious.

Almost as obvious as Mom's stubborn determination. Sure, she looks completely disinterested in some of these shots, pissed off at the world in others, but that drive is in her eyes. I bet nobody who knew her back then doubted that she'd get the hell out of Ivydell and never look back. Funny how some people just don't fit in the same place where others thrive.

Gran thrived here, but she was unique in her ability to adapt and create a full life wherever she landed. I love knowing she saw some of that in me, but she overestimated it. I'm nowhere near as adaptable as she was.

When I carry my cup to the counter for a refill, the wind has died down a little, and the now clearer view through my window makes me shake my head in disbelief. I step closer to take in the transformation.

Yesterday, the casita across the street was unoccupied.

Today, the curtains are open on the windows, and there is an SUV painted in a jewel-toned, tie-dyed pattern parked in the dirt driveway. Not a compact SUV either; we're talking full soccer mom cargo space. The tinted back windshield has a huge silver decal that says: Wild Love Jewelry. In slightly smaller letters underneath, it reads: Myrna Dankworth, Master Silversmith.

To the left, spanning the entire height of the glass, there's a logo that I'm sure could get you arrested in some states. Jailed for a substantial amount of time in a few. Not sure it wouldn't happen right here. Well, maybe not right here, but once you reach the paved road . . . yikes!

Who would drive around with that on their back window?

If I'd had anything stronger than coffee to drink, I wouldn't believe my eyes. There's no detail, like facial expressions or anything. In fact, the whole design is swirls and curlicues, but there is clearly a woman on all fours with her head thrown back. Behind her is a bear standing up on its back legs. Very close behind her. No visible bear schlong, but as close as they are, his invisible part would definitely be deep inside one of her invisible parts. Listen, his head is thrown back, too! There is definitely some burying of the bear banana going on there.

Finally, something happens here I want to share with Mom. The woman's an ER nurse. She's not shy about sharing the unusual things she's seen shoved in places they don't belong or the sex injuries that people seek treatment for, but I think this might shock even her. What if she knows this artist?

Maybe I'll keep it to myself for now.

Shit! There's a face staring back at me through the hazy space between our casitas. That must be her. Myrna Dankworth, master silversmith, purveyor of shiny obscenities. She's short enough that only part of her face is visible in the window—from the mouth up only, no sign of her chin—in her sixties, I'd guess, with sleek, shoulder-length white hair and heavy red glasses. No way to tell if her bob is dyed platinum or naturally white, but it's bright.

I wave. Because what else am I going to do? She knows I've seen it. She's seen me seeing it.

Where did she go?

Oh, she's coming outside. Whoa. She's so short she might've been standing on something at the window.

Crossing the street. Walking to my door. Knocking.

This is what I get for sticking my face in the window instead of minding my own business and going back to bed. I take a deep breath, try to smile in a way that doesn't seem forced, and open the door at a normal pace, not at all like someone who would rather be fucked by a bear than meet the woman standing on her doorstep.

Not literally, of course. Why was that the first thing I thought of? I don't want to have sex with a bear, I swear!

"Hi."

"Hi, there. I wasn't expecting to come home to a new neighbor. Saw your car when I pulled in last night." She extends her hand, because of course she does. I stare at it for a beat too long to go unnoticed, but it's a hand that fashions molesting bears. To be fair, I don't know that her depictions aren't meant to be consensual. First rule of Ivydell: don't ask.

"I'm Myrna." She shivers a little, and I realize she's not wearing a jacket. It's chilly out.

"I'm Ivy. Would you like to come in?"

"Well, of course." The diminutive woman is dressed all in red to match her glasses: red sweater, red leggings, red snakeskin ankle boots. A large, silver, filigree pendant hangs from a thick silver chain around her neck. I'm afraid to look too closely at it.

She steps inside and takes stock of my messy bed and small pile of dirty clothes in the corner. I don't know why I'm feeling ashamed of my lax housekeeping after seeing that logo on her window, but it feels like she's scrutinizing every inch of my space, her gaze ripe with judgment.

I'm slightly stunned by how impeccably put together she is—not at all what I'd expect from a woman who drives the madcap vehicle in her driveway.

"It smells like an herb garden in here. Petra's essential oils?"

"Yeah. I added some to my shampoo and conditioner." My hair is still damp, but it's dried a bit, and when it dries on its own with no product to tame it, it clumps into frizzy waves. Now I feel self-conscious about my living space and my hair.

"Hey, aren't you smart? I should try that. What's your story, Ivy?"

"I'm sorry?"

"Are you an artist, a medium, or an outlaw?"

"None of the above."

"Wow. A normie, huh? We haven't had one of those in Ivydell in a long time."

"I'm only here for a few months."

"Bad breakup?"

"No."

"You don't look like you're healing from any plastic surgery." Her eyes scan me from head to toe. "Liposuction maybe?"

"What? No."

"A journalist? You're not the first to try to infiltrate us so you can write some human-interest piece, but I can save you the trouble. We're not that interesting."

"I'm a graphic designer."

"Oh, so you lied. You are an artist."

"I don't think of myself as one."

She cocks her head. "How'd you hear about Ivydell?"

"My grandmother and my mom lived her before it was . . ." I'm not sure how to word it. I want to say disbanded because that's the word Gran always used, but Petra prefers to say stolen. "Before the oil and gas company laid claim to the land."

"Oh, way back in the before times. Yeah, those thieving dipshits thought we were just going to lie down and let them have Ivydell. Bunch of dumbass suits. Our lead attorney had hair down to his ass and a tattoo of a peace sign on one hand and a bull on the other. Boy, did they underestimate him."

So, she's been around long enough to have known Gran. And Mom.

"Patrice was my grandmother. Cecilia is my mom. You probably knew her as CiCi."

"Hot damn. I should've known by those eyes you were related to Patrice." Her smile spans the width of her face, but then it fades. "You said she *was* your grandmother? Is she gone, sweetie?"

"Six months ago." I don't know what to make of this woman who dresses like she should be an editor for Vogue or the owner of an art gallery, but talks and carries herself like she could manage a ranch.

She sees the open photo album on the table. "Past the age of ten, only Petra could call your mom CiCi. She'd correct anybody else right quick. She was a feisty little thing, but a sweetheart underneath it all. That's the age she was when I first arrived. I was in my mid-twenties and ready to burn down the status quo."

"She's still that way."

"Me, too."

The hell with not asking questions. I have to know. "Do you make jewelry that depicts women having sex with animals?"

"Not just women."

"Oh."

"Zoophilia has long been depicted in art and literature. I'm not suggesting people act on it, but there's some deep symbolism present in some of it."

"And the rest of it?"

"I don't kink shame, doll. I just give the people what they want."

"What's with the paint job on your car?"

"Oh, that's just for attention. And to piss people off."

"The logo, too?"

"No. I'm proud of the logo. That's art."

"Right. Would you like some coffee?"

"I'd love a cup."

As sexually symbolic bears are my witness, I don't care if the internet comes up all day.

Petra

Follow-Up Questions

I FINALLY GET UP the courage to invite Ivy over for dinner, fully prepare myself to talk about Patty with her for as long as she wants, and the first thing she hits me with is, "Did you ever see Gran again after they left Ivydell?"

It's the unavoidable follow-up questions that make me hesitate. But I said she could ask me anything. "Only once."

"She came back to visit?"

"No. I met her in Vegas."

Ivy does a spit take with her tea. "I can't imagine Gran in Vegas. How'd you convince her to meet you there, of all places?"

"It was her idea." I want to leave it at this, but we're going to get there, anyway. Might as well rip off the band-aid. "She wanted to confront your father. And I couldn't let her do that alone."

"Okay, for that, I could see her hopping a plane."

I can tell from her face that she's impressed that Patty went out there. I was, too.

"Mom got pregnant at eighteen. That was five years after they left Ivydell. Had you and Gran stayed in contact with each other all that time?"

"Not consistently. But when she called to say she was going to—and I quote—'rip the son-of-a-bitch's balls off with her bare hands,' I figured four hands were better than two."

Her eyes sparkle when she laughs. "So, my dad really was a famous Las Vegas magician. Wow. I tried looking him up online once, but I couldn't find anything."

"Famous? He did two shows a week at a rundown casino off the strip. His best illusion was making a naïve eighteen-year-old girl think he was more than he was."

"Was he tall?"

"Exceptionally tall. Handsome, too, though it pains me to admit it. He had a unique look about him, but he was common as dirt. Just another asshole who'd taken advantage of a girl too young and way too damn good for him. It only took Patty about fifteen minutes of screaming him into a corner to see that you and CiCi would both be better off without him. He was a coward, worried she'd come looking for money. As if he had any." I shrug and say it outright. "He was a loser."

"I can just imagine Gran screaming at some man she had to crane her neck to look up at with no fear at all. She could be the epitome of hell hath no fury."

"You don't have to tell me. I hear you met Myrna."

"Yeah. She's something, too."

"She's something all right." I spoon posole into her bowl. "The spirit sisters will probably come back soon. They're going to love you."

"What makes you say that?"

"You're CiCi's girl. Hell, Alma predicted you. Pissed Patty off to no end, but along you came, just the way Alma said you would."

"Okay, but a prediction isn't what created me."

"You know that and I know that. Doesn't change the fact that

Alma knew about you long before you were created."

"If you say so."

Ivy brings a spoonful of broth to her mouth, and I wonder if the spirit sisters will have any predictions for her.

Jensen

In the Desert in a House
with No Name

Ivy's silhouette in my headlights makes me smile. Her arm is raised like she's about to knock on my door. I don't know how she missed that my truck wasn't here. Never mind, yes, I do. She didn't notice it because she didn't bother to look for it.

She crosses her arms and waits for me to get out. When I reach the porch, she shoves two twenty-dollar bills at me.

"What's that for?"

"I want to look at the stars."

"And you want to pay me for an astronomy lesson?"

"No. I want to buy one of your good bottles of wine because I don't want to drive all the way to Hilltop tonight and I forgot to go earlier."

"You forgot, huh?"

"Yes. It was a clear day. I had a lot of work to catch up on. The next thing I knew, the sun was going down. And now I'm in the mood to drink wine and stare at the stars. So, will you sell me a bottle or not?"

"No." I step past her and open my door.

She marches in right behind me. "Oh, come on. Whatever I did to make you mad, I'm sorry. Don't be so petty. Sell me a bottle of wine."

"Put your damn money away. I'll give you a bottle of wine." I offer her a bottle of the same wine we drank with our picnic.

"Oh. Thanks. Are you going to help me drink it?"

"I haven't been invited."

"Will you say yes if I ask?"

"I don't know."

"Yes, you do. Don't make me ask if you're just going to say no, Stinger."

Ouch. I don't like her calling me that. "We're on a last name basis, now?"

"Well, you *are* wearing a shirt. I thought maybe it was a formal occasion."

"You're wearing pants with a zipper. I guess we're both in formal wear."

"I like leggings, okay? They're comfy. But these are nice jeans."

"They certainly look nice on you."

"Jensen James Stinger, you are cordially invited to spend the evening drinking wine and stargazing with Ivy Dell McAdams at Sparrow's Song. She requests the favor of a prompt RSVP."

She tilts her head, and a section of hair falls across her cheek. I immediately want to brush it back so I can see both her eyes.

"Mr. Stinger proposes a change of venue. He would like Ms. McAdams to join him at his residence instead." Her expression hardens. Why? My suggestion makes the most sense. We're already here. "He will provide snacks."

"Deal. What's the name of your place? You don't have a sign."

"It's the only one without a name."

"What? We have to give it one."

"You're not a permanent resident. You can't name a building."

"Show me where it says that in the official rules."

"My casita. My rules."

"Oh, please. I'll have this place named by the time the sun comes up."

Our eyes lock. That got awkward quick.

She holds the forty bucks out to me again. "I'd like to make an endowment to Ivydell in exchange for naming rights."

"Naming rights typically require a substantially larger donation."

"In Ivydell? I'm pretty sure forty bucks is twice the going rate."

"Fine. But I have final approval."

There's no way I'm taking that money from her, but I can't wait to see how many names she's willing to come up with.

"Are we celebrating something? Is that why you wanted better wine?"

"When you say better, it implies that I had any wine at all."

"Ah, the truth comes out."

"The truth was never hidden."

Maybe not that particular truth.

I open and pour the wine. She's already walked out onto my back patio. Through the open glass doors, I see her keep walking, and I know where she's headed.

When I built the pair of Adirondack chairs she's approaching, I definitely did it because I grew up sitting in them, both at the winery and at home. There are smaller chairs on my patio, but the Adirondacks are set further out. They provide a better spot for stargazing. That's not why I put them there, though. They're heavy enough not to blow away, and I wanted a spot to sit where I could feel the wind all around me. No wall at my back. One familiar good thing.

Sinking into the chair next to hers, I let muscle memory guide me. It takes over, and my back and legs relax against the wood. The wine floods my tongue, and I savor it for a few seconds. It reminds me of sitting with her on my tailgate. The way she popped olives into her mouth like they were candy. Strands of her hair glimmering in the sunlight. Me wanting to spend the whole day with her—until the bars came down so unexpectedly. I can't even explain it to myself.

The gist of it isn't a mystery, but there's no logic to the timing or the magnitude of what I felt. It still hits out of the blue sometimes. But she didn't deserve to be iced out like that.

Thank goodness for wine. If she hadn't wanted a convenient bottle, she wouldn't be here.

"Do you feel safe sitting out here like this?" She pulls her feet up to the edge of her seat.

"Yeah, but honestly, I think it's less about feeling safe than it is the lack of worrying about my safety. Worry doesn't sit with me here. My mind lets go and I can just be."

"I'm not sure I've ever felt that way."

"Give my chairs a chance to work their magic." I smile at her.

"Did you make these?"

"I built them, yes."

"Make, build, it's the same thing."

Her defensiveness snaps into place like a reflex. I can't help but wonder if it's a general trait or I'm the catalyst.

"I didn't mean to correct you. Just a preference for one word over the other." I'm prone to a little defensiveness, too, I guess. I open the music app on my phone. "Any requests?"

"Whatever badgers don't like, I'm good with."

"They hate this song."

"Then I love it." Her head tilts back, and she looks to the sky. "I've only seen this many stars in pictures."

"No romantic ex that took you on exotic vacations?"

"I'm not big on romance. Prefer to keep it real."

"You don't think romance can be real?"

"I don't need a bunch of performative bullshit done just because it's what a man thinks he's supposed to do. Like it's an obligation. I'd rather he be himself and only do what he wants to do."

"Nobody wants anybody to be fake, but give me an example of something you think men only do because we think we're supposed to."

"Most of the showy stuff is done begrudgingly. Flowers. Gifts. Exotic vacations."

"You feel like no man has ever given you something because he sincerely wanted to? Never your favorite flowers to celebrate something? Nothing bought on a whim because it made him think of you? No careful thought put into a birthday or Christmas present?"

"Gifts make me suspicious. I don't like to be manipulated."

"Damn. You've got some deep trust issues."

"Maybe I've just got a good head on my shoulders."

"You've never been in love?"

"I thought I was a few times, but looking back? Not so much. I'm not a fan of the mushy stuff, anyway."

What does that mean? She doesn't like to snuggle? Hates compliments?

"You're speaking in generalities. Be specific. Tell me one mushy thing you don't like."

"Okay. I hate it when people call sex making love."

"Why?"

"Because I don't think sex needs flowery language. It's a physical act that can be great for what it is. We don't have to pretend there has to be some deep emotional attachment for it to be worth-while."

"I enjoy a hot, satisfying fuck as much as anybody else, but you know sex can be more than that. Not that it can't still be raw and dirty with someone you care about, but it's different when there's more between you. What does it hurt if people want to call it something different when it is?"

"Is it though?"

"You really don't believe a man has ever made love to you? Not one experience that you'd classify as making love?"

"Can we change the subject, please?"

"Sure."

I'll just let the question spin in my own fucking mind forever. Who hurt her? And why do I want to feel his jaw break under my boot? Whoever he was, I hope another woman hurts him far worse than he hurt Ivy, leaves him broken and miserable like he deserves. I'd still like to kick the shit out of him.

She gasps, and my eyes scan the surrounding terrain, looking for whatever animal she's seen.

"Did you see that?"

"What did it look like?"

"Falling stars. There was more than one." Her voice sounds like a kid who's caught Santa in her living room.

"Meteor shower. We might see more."

"Do they happen all the time?"

"No, but they're not rare. You can actually look up the schedule. I figured you knew there was one happening, and that's why you wanted to watch the stars tonight."

"I just wanted to zone out and stare at something beautiful for a while."

Her features look softer, bathed in moonlight. She looks back toward the stars, her eyes wide in anticipation of more streaks in the sky.

How can a woman who gets so excited about prairie dogs and shooting stars be so damn hard?

I want to make her feel things she's never felt before. Make her believe. Make every wish she's ever made on a star come true. These thoughts are all too dangerous for me to entertain, so I zone out and stare at something beautiful for a while instead. Pretend I don't want more than I can handle.

Ivy

Stars Fall

"I was promised snacks."

My first meteor shower made me hungry. Plus, I didn't eat dinner. And the temperature is falling fast out here.

Jensen stands and offers me a hand. I let him pull me up. Let him warm me with a kiss. His tongue tastes like wine, and the way he moves it in my mouth paints memories of him using it somewhere else. His casita should probably have a filthy name.

He lights a fire in his fireplace, taking his time to do it right, just like when he lit mine. But I wasn't about to starve then. Right now, I think a half-ass fire would be fine.

"Do you have popcorn?"

"Yeah." He keeps warming the chimney.

I open his pantry door and stare in amazement at the level of his organization. My eyes skate over the shelves, searching for the box of popcorn, but the only boxes I see are a few rice mixes and some Japanese bread crumbs. Maybe he takes the bags out and stacks them? All I find are cans and jars.

"I don't see popcorn in here."

His shadow gets heavier on the wall next to me until I can feel his body heat pressed against my back. He reaches above my head, and his hand brings down a jar from the top shelf. He rattles the loose popcorn in front of my face.

"What are you, a pioneer? Why don't you buy microwave popcorn? It cooks in less than two minutes."

"Because it's full of chemicals and it tastes bad." He sets a saucepan on the stove and rests the lid on the counter. It takes some adjusting to get the flame of the burner where he wants it.

"Are you sure that's enough oil?" It doesn't look like enough to me.

"How many times have you made popcorn on the stove, Ivy?"

"Never."

"Then you've never actually had popcorn."

"Are you calling me a popcorn virgin? What about theater popcorn?"

"Oh, damn. I didn't know you were a popcorn slut."

"It's true. When the mood hits, any popcorn will do. I've had it from the microwave, the concessions counter, the snack aisle in the grocery store . . ."

He pours kernels into the pan and puts the lid on, giving it a good shake before he turns and grabs my hips, pulling me into him and letting his scruff tickle my cheek as his warm, husky whisper fills my ear. "Well, tonight I'm going to give you the best you've ever had."

Sir! My panties were not built for your popcorn innuendo.

A chill runs down the back of my neck, making me shiver. My nipples knot at the sensation, and when he takes his cheek from mine and steps back, his eyes go straight to them. I know they're hard because I could feel the response, but I'm wearing a bra. He can't possibly know my nipples are hard, but his salacious grin confirms he does. *Note to self: quit tossing the liners when they come out in the dryer.*

"Damn, you do get excited about popcorn."

I'm not shy about my body—I grew up in bikinis that went from little girl cute to teenager skimpy to grown-ass woman micro—but I feel my shoulders round a little. It's not actual insecurity, and it's damn sure not because I don't want his attention. It's a reflex, not an unwelcome one, but one that hasn't been triggered in a long time.

I used to enjoy suggestive flirtations, but I'm out of practice. Somewhere along the way, this level of flirting became unnecessary. An obsolete step. Jensen Stinger doesn't skip steps.

The first kernel pops, and he turns his attention away from me to shake the pan again. A few more explode, and the unmistakable smell seeps out in the steam that's escaping around the lid. Nothing else smells like popcorn. I inhale and relish this moment.

More kernels explode, sounding off in a steady cadence now. The pan fills with fluffy goodness. He steps away to open his little fridge. I sneak a glimpse inside. It's pretty full, definitely not just beer and condiments.

"I hope you like a lot of butter."

"Not too much."

"Why am I even letting you weigh in on this? You don't know how much you like because you've never had real popcorn before."

"Yeah, you keep saying that."

He sets a stick of butter on the counter and turns off the burner. The popping sounds slow as he takes two bowls from a cabinet and a knife from a drawer. The smaller bowl gets half the stick of butter before it goes into the microwave. Once the butter melts, he removes the lid from the pan and dumps the popcorn into the large bowl. He adds salt and uses his hands to mix it before he pours on the butter and repeats the mixing.

Wiping his salty, buttery hands on a kitchen towel, he nods at the bowl. "Go ahead. Try it."

I take a single piece of popcorn as if I'm wary of it, but I already know I'm going to like it. Extending my tongue, I set the morsel on the tip and pull it into my mouth. Oh, damn, that's good popcorn. I take several pieces and put them into my mouth all at once so I can really taste it. My eyes roll back in my head.

"How dare you complicate my life like this? I was perfectly happy tossing a bag into the microwave. Now, it's going to take me five times as long to make popcorn, and I'm going to have to wash dishes!"

"The best things in life are worth a little extra effort." He grabs a fistful of popcorn and feeds it into his mouth like his hand is a funnel.

There's a buttery sheen on his bottom lip that's too enticing to resist. When I step closer to taste his popcorn kiss, it instantly erases all my best kiss memories, like this is my first. Like I've never really been kissed before.

And then he deepens it, sinks one hand into my hair and presses the other into the small of my back, pulling me against him.

This concoction of salt and butter and wine should be a lip balm flavor. But it would need a warning on the label: Prolonged use may create a Pavlovian response in your pussy every time you hear a popcorn kernel burst.

I let him end the kiss. He picks up the popcorn bowl. "Come here," he says. But he doesn't mean for me to come back to where I was. He walks toward his bed and sets the popcorn on the mattress, and then he goes to the bathroom and turns on the light, pulling the door almost closed so it only emits a sliver of glow when he turns out all the other lights, including the lamp next to his bed.

Standing in front of me, he stacks his pillows against the head-board, and then he frees a button on his shirt. "We're going to take off all our clothes and climb onto this bed. You're going to sit against these pillows so you can eat your popcorn while you watch the sky through the patio doors and wish on any shooting stars you see, even if they're meteors." He winks.

"What are you going to be doing?"

"Licking your sweet pussy until you see stars in this room. Until you're rocking against my mouth and gasping for air." He frees his last button, peels his shirt off, and drops it onto the floor. "Until it's time to make love to you."

I feel the sound of his zipper from the top of my spine all the way down.

"I might need some water."

He brings me a glass of water and my refilled wine glass, and sets them both on the nightstand next to the propped pillows, sliding them close to the edge to be sure they'll be within reach. "I don't want any of your needs to go unmet, but you're still dressed, and that doesn't meet either of our needs, does it?"

I pull my sweater over my head quickly because he's sitting on the edge of the bed with his jeans flayed open at his hips, pulling off his boots, and I don't want to block my view for any longer than I absolutely have to. My bra strap flies apart when I unhook it as if had been under pressure. It meets my sweater on his floor.

When I sit next to him to take off my boots, he stands and lifts my leg until my foot is right under his ribs. He removes my boots and socks. And then he pulls me back up to my feet and opens my button and zipper to match his. Our jeans hit the cool tiles under our feet together.

He lifts me and gently sets me on the bed with the pillows at my back. Moving the popcorn closer to me, he says, "Get comfortable."

While I settle into place, he crawls between my legs and nuzzles his face against my inner thigh, planting kisses before he pushes my legs wider. He teases his tongue under the stretched triangle of satin that barely covers me now, his fingers joining to tug on the material until it slips between my seam, pulling harder to agitate my clit enough to make me squirm.

His groan is barely audible, but it makes me sink lower on the mattress. "Don't waste that popcorn. I worked hard on it."

"Are you trying to make me choke? Is this how you kill women and make it look like an accident?"

"That's the last thing I want to do to you."

"Well, yeah, it would be the last thing anyone ever did to me. I hope."

He laughs. "Go ahead. Get all that deflecting with humor out of your system." He pushes my panties inside me with two fingers, fucking the slick fabric into me until it's thoroughly soaked. "Because I've never wanted a woman more seriously."

Pulling the satin back to the surface and to the side, he spreads my juices over my skin, letting his tongue follow.

There's no way I could eat anything while he does this, but I take a sip of water. A larger sip of wine. As I reach to set the glass back down, a blue-white streak flashes in my peripheral vision. Probably just a nerve response to his mouth closing over my opening, his nose brushing my clit. But I close my eyes and make a wish, just in case.

I don't know if the meteor shower is still happening or single stars are falling because opening my eyes again would require more control over my body than I currently possess. It belongs to him right now.

His powerful hands grip tighter between my ass and thighs when they quiver, letting me know he's got me. He'll support me while he pushes me over the edge. Hold me while I ride it out. While I rock against his mouth just the way he said I would. Gasping for air. Wishing it didn't have to end.

Before the aftershocks subside, his body blankets mine, warming me while his kisses pull me under faster than any riptide ever could. I want to drown in him. He trails his mouth down my neck, and goosebumps prickle my arms. His hot tongue traces my areola, enhancing the contraction of the stiff peak at the center.

When he draws my erect nipple into his mouth and sucks so exquisitely hard, his tongue still lavishing warmly across it, every action of his mouth causes a reaction in my pussy, as if it's an instrument he can play from either point.

My unconscious humming rises to a moan when his heavy cock pushes inside me. His hips thrust in small circles and his mouth returns to mine. He pins my wrists above my head and drives deeper, grinding like he's trying to go through me, his kiss becoming ferocious. Animalistic.

He slows, and I match his rhythm while our shallow breaths deepen together as well. Separating his mouth from mine, he lifts his face to look at me. "You feel so damn good. Taste amazing, smell incredible. You are fucking addictive, Ivy Dell McAdams."

I smile up at him. "Just Ivy."

"Nothing about you is just."

"Shut up and make love to me."

His kiss is intoxicating, his lovemaking is savagely sweet, and his feral groans when he comes render me helpless under him like a marionette whose strings have been cut. I know as soon as it's happened that he's severed me from something I wasn't ready to be rid of. Something already too far gone to claw back.

"We don't even know each other, Jensen. What the hell are we doing?"

"I don't know. But let's keep doing it until we figure it out."

Jensen

Tightening Connections

THE SPIRIT SISTERS FIND me lying on my back, replacing the water supply valve on Myrna's toilet. They didn't text to ask where I was, just showed up. I'm sure Petra told them I was over here, but it always unnerves me when they appear without warning. I didn't even know they were back in Ivydell.

I don't stand to greet them because I just got everything lined up straight and I'm in the middle of connecting it. Everybody has some sort of repair that needs doing when they first get back. I'll be busy for the next few weeks as the seasonal residents file in.

"Welcome back, ladies. Do you have a list for me?"

Alma clears her throat. "No, Dear."

"We have a message for you," Elma says.

"You've got clients scheduled already?" I know that's probably not what she meant, but I don't want to think about the other possibility. They've offered me readings again and again, and I've always turned them down. But they've never specifically said they had a message for me.

Whatever it is, I don't want to hear it, but I also don't want to hurt their feelings. And it's not because I'm afraid of them. A little cautious, sure, but who wouldn't be?

"Not yet, but we'll be taking appointments soon."

"The spirits won't be here until next week."

Oh, good. They have an itinerary.

"We're ladies of leisure for a few days."

Okay, maybe they didn't mean what I thought they did. If the spirits aren't even here—

Alma's voice is slightly higher pitched than Elma's, and I've been able to tell them apart when they speak for a few years now. "She says to tell you good acid."

'Moderate-plus." Elma chuckles, as if she knows what that means. "Perhaps even a unicorn."

My hand slips on the wrench, and I bust my knuckle on the bolt I've been tightening. I squeeze my eyes shut to keep from cussing, and the moment I do, I may as well have blacked out.

"IF YOU DON'T TELL my parents that you can't keep working so many hours, I will." I roll another swath of the wall with the bright blue paint she's chosen. She should rest on her only day off, but she insisted on helping me paint the garage I've converted into a billiards room. This is the final coat. It looks so much better than the gray I'd originally picked out.

"Dad is going to work you to death if you don't put your foot down with him. It's what he does. He uses people up."

"My exam is next month. The stress will be gone. I'll officially be a sommelier, and it will have all been worth it." She extends her roller to conjoin the sections of wall we're painting. She's closing in the last gap. "I'm pretty sure I'll survive until then."

"You better."

"If I died, you'd replace me with another beautiful sommelier in no time." She flings her dark hair dramatically. I laugh at the fact that she's somehow gotten paint on the back of her head.

"No way. You'd haunt me."

"If you were lucky, I would." She touches her paint roller to my chest, leaving a wide blue smudge on my skin. "I'd probably be your wing woman from the beyond, coming back to rate your dates, scaring them off if they were all wrong for you."

"And you'd probably use snobby wine terms, so I wouldn't even know what you meant half the time."

"You'd know. If I said she had good acid or was moderate-plus, what would that mean?"

"It would mean you liked her just fine."

"Right. She's good, and she might even get better, but if I called her a unicorn . . ."

"That won't happen." I set my roller on the tray, and then take hers and lay it on from the opposite end. Pulling her against me, I smear the blue paint from my chest onto her tee shirt.

"It might."

"No, a man only finds one unicorn in his life. And I already found mine."

"OH, NO. YOU'RE BLEEDING." Alma practically climbs me, trying to see my hand.

"We distracted him and he got hurt." Now Elma descends on

me. "This is all our fault. We should've waited until he was done."

All I can see when I open my eyes fully are their matching concerned faces, leaning in way too close.

"I'm fine. It's just a scrape."

They retreat, giving me some much-needed room to breathe.

What the fuck just happened?

The hairs on my arms stand straight on end. It's not nice to call eccentric old women creepy, but crazy doesn't sound any kinder, and those are the only two choices that come to mind.

"Put some of Petra's salve on that."

"We have a fresh jar if you're in need."

I shake my head. "Thanks, but I think I have some." My words come out rushed as I sit up. "It's fine. Really."

The sisters exchange a glance and a nod. Thankfully, they don't ask if I understood the message, or worse, repeat it. They leave quietly. I drop my head between my knees, hoping the room will stop spinning soon so I can finish this job and call it a day.

Ivy

The Feeling Comes Back

THE BUZZING OF MY phone echoes off the bathroom counter again, but I'm not getting out of the shower to check notifications. Mom can wait. Why is she panicking? We just talked last night.

Shampoo runs into my eyes, and I move my face into the spray before turning around to rinse my hair. Another buzz. I massage my conditioner down to the ends of my hair, and shave my legs while it soaks in.

It feels decadent to spend this much time enjoying the steam carrying the essential oils, to breathe it in. I stand under the water until the heat fades, shutting it off right before it goes cold. I've been grabbing quick showers for the past few days because I didn't wash my hair, but it couldn't wait another day. After all the wind we've had, I felt like I probably had a pound of dust on my head.

I needed a long, hot shower for more than cleansing my hair and body, though. Whenever I need to think, really think about something, there's nothing better than filling my lungs with steam and letting the hot water hit me. At home, the water pressure in my apartment is so good that if I turn it all the way up, I feel like I'm being hydro blasted. And I love that. Here, it's more like somebody put their thumb over the end of a hose, but it's better than nothing. At least it gets hot.

When I met Jensen, if someone had told me I'd be thinking about him in the shower, I'd have envisioned a whole different scenario. Today, it was deep thoughts, not fantasies—thoughts that should've helped me make sense of things, but didn't. All that shower did was steal my energy. I'm drained and I haven't even sat down to work yet.

With a towel wrapped around my body, I open the bathroom door to let the steam out, yawn, and pick up my phone. Six missed text messages, but they're not from Mom. A quick scan down my screen confirms they're all from Zara.

I squeeze my eyes shut as soon as I see her name. Shit! Did I miss an early morning meeting? If I missed two meetings in a row, I'll be in a private meeting before the day's out. I take a breath, open my eyes, and start reading.

> *WTF? There's a mountain lion on the loose where you are?*

I forgot I posted about that.

> *Did they catch it?*

> *Girl, you better reply.*

> *IVY!!!!!! You can't just say there's a wild animal roaming around and then disappear!*

In my defense, I've been preoccupied since then.

> *I'm starting to panic. You know how I get when I panic. Why would you do this to me?*

> *So help me, Ivy! I will send the cops out to you!*

Where is she going to send them? All she knows is that I'm somewhere in the west Texas desert. I laugh, but I feel bad that she's worried. Our team lead could confirm I've been online for work. Proof of life. But she wants it to come from me, which is fair. She's being a good friend, and I've been a pretty bad one lately.

> *I'm fine. No more mountain lion sightings. I'm safe and sound. Just been busy.*

> *Too busy to post? Who are you and what have you done with Ivy?*

> *Busy with a man . . . does that help?*

> *I need a picture. And his full name. If you go missing, I need to know who to point the finger at!*

> *I don't have a pic. Jensen James Stinger. 29 years old. From Napa Valley. Scorpion tattoo on the left side of his collarbone.*

> *Greenish eyes. Light brownish hair. Not too long, but not short. Kinda shaggy. Never wears a shirt.*

> *Very good with his hands.*

> *I might need more than one pic.*

For the first time since I came here, I feel like maybe more than one person should know where I'm actually at. What if something happened to Mom? I should've given more people specifics.

> *I'll see what I can do. For the record, I'm at a place called Ivydell. Just in case.*

> *Wait a damn minute! Your middle name is Dell. Why is there a desert named after you?*

> *This place isn't named after me. I'm named after it. Not the whole desert. Just this small section of it.*

> *Bring me a keychain.*

She thinks there's a gift shop. I try to imagine what she must see in her head as Ivydell. She probably thinks it's a resort, a secluded spa with hot springs and a chef. No one could imagine this place. Maybe one of the artists will sell keychains during the festival.

Why is this place called Ivydell?

I've never wondered, but now I'm consumed with the question. I haven't seen any ivy growing wild. Maybe it pops up in the spring? I look up dell because who even knows what that means?

Huh. That fits even less than ivy.

I run a comb through my hair and get dressed as quickly as I can, stepping into my shoes on my way out the door.

Petra is across the road talking to Myrna. I walk over, intending to say hi and ease myself into their conversation, but the words shoot out of my mouth like they've been launched from a cannon. "Why is this place called Ivydell? There is no ivy. It's not a dell. What the hell?"

Myrna lifts a mug with her still-disturbing-to-me logo on it up to her mouth and sips. Steam shrouds her face, and she inhales. Kindred spirit. But she doesn't answer my question.

"Good morning." Petra smiles at me the way people do when they're gently trying to let you know you just acted like an ass, but they know it was an accident.

I don't mean to be so hard-charging. It only happens when I have a burning question or a spectacular solution to something or a brilliant suggestion or . . . okay, it happens a lot. But it's not my whole personality. I can be calm, just not when I'm excited.

"Sorry. Good morning. I didn't mean to barge over and interrupt, but the question is going to drive me mad."

"Nobody knows." Petra shakes her head as if it's a terrible shame.

Myrna laughs.

Two older women walk toward us. I don't know where they came from, but I know who they are with one look. They wear matching purple down vests over bright green sweaters, and they move in sync. Their silver hair is in a single long braid down their backs and their faces are carbon copies. These are the spirit sisters. I'm never in a million years going to learn how to tell them apart.

Petra waves to welcome them.

They're smiling as they approach. Are they staring at me?

Alma introduces herself first. She doesn't offer her hand, the first non-handshaker I've met in Ivydell. Elma's voice is unique, and I think it might be their only distinction from one another.

"Hi, I'm Ivy."

"We know," Alma says, still smiling at me.

"She has her grandmother's eyes." Elma looks to Petra when she says it.

"Her nature, too." Petra shoves her hands in her jacket pockets and rocks back on her heels.

"Indeed, she does." Alma and Elma nod in agreement.

They just met me. They can't know . . . ohhhhh. The air is still, but I swear I feel a breeze blow over me, not the harsh unforgiving winds we've had since I got her, but a gentler, comforting swish of air across my face as if a fan has oscillated in my direction.

The sisters say they're afraid someone named Belle won't be coming back.

"Damn," Petra says. No questions asked. She takes their statement as fact, doesn't ask if they've talked to Belle or if she sent them a message. Petra struck me as the no-nonsense type as soon as I met her, but she appears to be all in for the nonsense of Alma and Elma.

I'm trying to keep an open mind, but I have questions. And I'm probably not supposed to ask them. Ivydell may not have a lot of rules, but I really hate that one.

Myrna shakes her head. "She'll be missed, that's for sure."

"Her absence will be felt, but she seemed to be in a positive state of mind when she called." Elma watches a hawk soar above us. "She's struggling with some health issues. Says she hopes to return next year."

"We feel certain she will."

Okay, so they got a phone call. Not a psychic message from a dead woman. Just because they claim to channel spirits doesn't mean they can't still communicate like the rest of us. Or like the rest of us did twenty years ago, I guess. At any rate, I feel suddenly much more comfortable around them.

I listen as the women discuss other part-time residents of Ivydell, ones they're looking forward to seeing and a few who they hope won't come until the last minute. It's a cohesive community, but there's always at least one person who's harder to get along with than the rest. Sometimes, Ivydell doesn't seem so different from anywhere else.

The sisters say they need to get back to their walk, and Petra and Myrna nod like they know some secret significance of Alma and Elma taking a walk, so I do the same.

As they walk past me, Alma says, "Geraldine was the one who named Ivydell."

Elma adds. "A name to remind her of the place she would miss while she was in the place she had to be."

The same breeze from earlier whispers through the baby hairs drying at my temples. They had to have been close enough to hear me ask about the name. That's how they knew. But I didn't see them when I crossed the road to head over to Myrna's. Maybe I've already gotten out of the habit of looking both ways. It's not like there's any traffic here.

We all turn toward the roar of Cujo's motorcycle. He slows before he passes us, a welcome mercy because it minimizes the amount of dirt he'll stir up. Josephine hops off the back of the bike as soon as he stops in front of her casita, and jogs over to join us. Cujo rides off like he was her hired driver. No goodbye kiss, not so much as two words exchanged between them.

She offers a general hello, and then zeroes in on me. "You wanna do something today?"

"I'm supposed to work, but I could avoid it for a few more hours. What'd you have in mind?"

"I could give you a tattoo."

"What was your second choice?"

"We could go for a hike. I know a great spot."

Part of me wants to say yes to this, even though I just showered. I've been way too sedentary since I got here. But visions of mountains lions dance in my head. It occurs to me I'd probably say yes to a hike if Jensen asked, and the confliction I feel is distressing.

Why do I have to feel safer with him? He doesn't have any special mountain lion defenses.

"Not really feeling up for a hike. Is there a third option?"

"We could just hang out and talk."

"Let's go with that one."

We leave Petra and Myrna to their coffee and roadside chat. They don't rush us off, but I think they're glad to see us go so they can get back to their original conversation.

Josephine opens her front door without putting a key in the lock.

"You don't lock your front door?"

"Nobody does that here."

"I do."

"You're a short-timer." She flings her bag onto her bed. "And you have colossal trust issues, so, of course, you lock your door."

"Jensen said that about me, too."

"Well, I guess he would know." She pulls cups off a shelf. "Coffee?"

"Please." I sit at her table with my chin in my hands. "Why did you say that? He doesn't really know me."

"He's spent the most time with you."

"Not really." Has he? Shit. She's right. I came here on a mission, and I've spent more time with him than with Petra.

"You think he's wrong?" Her coffee already smells strong, and all she's done is open the canister.

I collapse my arms onto the table and hang my head. "No. I know he's right. You're right. Y'all are right, okay?" Why does everybody keep being right about me here?

"Okay. I wasn't trying to insult you. Just stating a fact. Wanna talk about the cause?"

"Of what?"

"Your trust issues. What was his name?"

"You mean *their* names?"

"Damn. You got fucked over in poly relationship?"

She might be the only person I know who would've jumped to that conclusion. No, she definitely is. "No. I'm a slow learner who is apparently prone to repeating my mistakes."

"You had a type, huh?"

"Is controlling asshole who turns out to be an insecure fuckboy a type?"

"The very worst type. You dated that type back-to-back?"

"Straight from the arms of one to the other. I'm not an idiot, but I definitely played one for a while."

"And then you swore off relationships and vowed to stay single."

"That sounds like experience talking."

"Yeah. Smart women. Dumb choices. It happens."

She sets a cup of coffee in front of me, followed by a carton of vanilla creamer.

"I know. Doesn't make it any less humiliating when it happens."

"Of course not, but eventually, you reach a point where it's far enough in the past that you don't feel defined by it anymore, and you move on."

"Is that what you're doing with Cujo?" I stir creamer into my coffee.

"There is a much simpler definition for what I'm doing with Cujo."

"And you're happy with that?"

"Yeah, it works for me." She studies me for a minute before she says, "I'm not against committed relationships. I just don't know that I'm built for that life."

"Me either."

Her face morphs into the universal expression of *are you fucking kidding me right now*? "You may not be ready for it, babe, but I'm pretty sure you are custom built for it. And that's okay."

"No, it's actually not. I don't want to get married, buy a house on a cul-de-sac, and become a mom who chaperones school field trips. I want a more fulfilling life than that."

"For some people, that is a fulfilling life. But you can share any kind of life you want with someone. It doesn't have to be that."

"It's always that. People say it'll be different for them, and then that's where they end up."

"Any woman who shows up here the way you did doesn't seem destined for that kind of life to me. But you do come across like the committed relationship type. You just need an actual grown partner who wants the same kind of different as you."

"Is there something in the water here that makes people think they instantly know someone?"

"The only thing in the water here is too many minerals. It'll wreck your hair. And your skin."

"Well, I've got that to look forward to."

"Good moisturizer and conditioner and you'll be fine." She grabs some pretzels from her pantry and a container of strawberry cream cheese from her fridge. "Breakfast of champions."

We drag pretzels through the pink cream cheese and continue to shift the conversation toward lighter topics.

When I say I have to leave, she asks if I'm doing okay in Ivydell.

"Yeah. I get anxious sometimes, but that's nothing new for me. At home, putting my bare feet in grass or the sand on the beach helps. Wading in the water while the waves rush in. None of that is an option here."

"Putting your bare feet against the earth is grounding, no matter what they rest on. Sand is just another kind of dirt. We've got dirt."

"True. Thanks. I'll give that a try later when I'm done working."

"Sure. Or you could go see if Stinger feels like fucking. That might do wonders for your anxiety, too."

"I thought personal stuff was supposed to stay personal here."

"You're just not supposed to ask about it. I didn't ask about anything. You, however, did ask me about Cujo."

"You didn't have to answer."

"Fair enough. Start thinking about what kind of tattoo you want because I'm definitely giving you one before you leave here."

It's not a far walk to Jensen's unnamed casita. Or the shop, where he's probably hanging out shirtless. A walk will probably do me good. I need some exercise and to put my feet against the earth. Two birds, one stone. If Alma and Elma feel safe walking around Ivydell, there's no reason I shouldn't.

Even with all the dirt, the air feels cleaner here in a way that defies explanation. No salt weighing it down, I guess. But I love salt air. This is nice, though. Different, but good. I wish I'd taken more snow-covered cactus pics. It was pretty while it lasted. Peaceful. Melted sooner than I expected. I didn't realize that might've been the last snowfall. Maybe there will be some blooms before I have to leave. I'll definitely get pictures of that. And the chipmunks.

Jensen is on his phone inside the shop when I walk up. I wave through the window and he motions to let me know he'll be done in five.

I slip my shoes off and carry them on my fingertips as I wander away from the building a bit to give him some privacy. Don't want him to think I'm eavesdropping.

Desert dirt under my feet feels nothing like walking on the beach or through the lush grass in the park. I'm not sure I could get used to this, but the logic of it being the earth, regardless, is sound. I put my one foot in front of the other and block out everything outside this moment in time.

The blood-curdling scream that comes from my mouth on my next step is beyond my control. Jensen flies out of the shop with his head pivoting until he sees me. He runs over and scoops me up in his arms.

"I think I stepped on a nail. A nail on fire. Maybe a razor blade. On fire. That was dipped in acid first." I can't unflex my ankle. The pain is paralyzing. Tears roll down my cheeks, and I'm scared to look down, afraid of what I might see sticking out of my foot.

He carries me to his truck and sets me on the hood so he can inspect my injury. "Well, the good news is that it wasn't a nail or a razor blade. But we're about to find out if you're allergic to scorpions."

"How long is it going to hurt like this?"

"It'll ease up soon. Might still hurt for an hour. Give or take." He slides me off the hood back into his arms and carries me toward his house. "But it's going to be sore for a while. It might go numb."

"Forever?"

"No. The feeling will come back."

He sets me on his kitchen counter facing the sink so he can wash my foot. I think I would've fit fine on the bathroom counter, but the stinging sensation overrides any desire to question his choice. Once he's dried my foot, he carries me to his bed and props pillows under my ankle. When he goes back to the kitchen, I hear ice being put in a bag. He brings paper towels and a roll of duct tape back with the ice, along with a pain reliever and some water.

While I swallow the tablet, he presses the bag to the sole of my foot and wraps paper towels around my entire foot until it looks like a mummy, and then he secures his wrap with duct tape to hold the ice in place.

It's the most *man bandage* ever. It still hurts like fire, but I have to snap a pic for Mom. I'll send it later after I'm sure I'm not allergic.

"This is far less pleasant than the last time I was propped on your pillows," I laugh, but it's slight.

"I could do that for you now, but I'm not sure how much good it would do."

I laugh harder. "It's the thought that counts."

So much for working today. I should be much more upset about the thought of another lost day, but I honestly don't care. I'm sure it's the toxins and the pain clouding my judgment. My hours are flex and I'm not on a pressing deadline for anything, but it's not like me to just not give a shit about my job.

Jensen plants a soft kiss on my forehead. "Do you like to be held when you're in pain or left alone?"

"I've never felt this exact pain before, but I think being held might be good."

He helps me sit up so he can slide in behind me, and then he pulls me back against his chest with his thighs framing mine.

"It'll be all better in an hour?" I ask.

I feel his body tense before he answers. "Give or take. Tell me about growing up at the beach."

"You're from California. You've been to beaches. Tell me about growing up where you did."

"I'm sure you've been to wineries."

"Yeah, but I didn't grow up with a vineyard in my backyard."

"How about we swap stories? You tell me a story about how you grew up, and then I'll tell you one about me."

"Okay. I ran track for two years in high school, and we trained on the beach. Every morning, we had to run in the sand, and we weren't supposed to run near the water where it was hard packed and level. Our coach didn't run with us. He'd come along randomly in a golf cart to check up on us. Everybody used to veer closer to the water when he wasn't watching, but he'd catch me every time. I think to this day, he probably believes I did it every time he drove off."

"Did you?"

"I really didn't. But I never got faster, no matter how much loose sand I ran through. I'm just a slow runner. I would've never made the track team in a bigger school."

"So, you didn't run anchor in the relay."

"Compared to my teammates, I ran like I was attached to an anchor."

His chest shakes under me as he laughs.

At first, he says it wasn't actually fun to grow up on a vineyard because when he was little he couldn't play in it, and when he was older, he had to work in it. When I press him to tell me one fun thing he remembers doing there, he thinks for a few minutes, and then he smiles.

"Okay, so I wasn't supposed to play in the vines, and I for sure wasn't supposed to take my friends into them, but I had a collection of remote-controlled monster trucks and that was the best place to drive them, so we'd sneak and do it. The best part was the workers would never tell on us. They'd watch out for us, make sure we didn't get caught."

I can't tell which he enjoyed more, racing the trucks through the vines or getting away with it.

When I ask him to tell me another story, he does. I tell him a little about the differences in town during the off-season and summer, and then ask him to tell me how old he was when he started working in the vineyards, and ask him questions to spur him to tell me something else before I share again. He lets me pry. I know he's humoring me because of the scorpion sting, but I'm not ashamed to take advantage of it.

He rubs my arms as we share our stories. This is such an unexpected way to spend the day. If not for the burning and tingling in my foot, it would be perfect. Outside this space, I have adult responsibilities that I'm completely ignoring. I'm not on vacation, but I am.

I know now that I'm not allergic to scorpions, that Jensen has some amazing memories of growing up on a vineyard, that he keeps them under wraps until they're coaxed out of him, and that I really love listening to him talk.

Jensen

We All Scream for Ice Cream

I STOP BY IVY's on my way back from helping Dice replace his water heater. He needed company more than help. He's about to head out, and I could've replaced it for him while he was gone, but I didn't suggest it when he asked me to come over. I learned a long time ago he likes to hang out for a few hours before he leaves for a tournament. Maybe it puts him in the right headspace, or it could just be a superstition thing. Hard to figure out a gambler.

If Ivy's working, I shouldn't interrupt her. I know she's struggling to work while she's here, and not just because of our less-than-ideal internet. But it's only been a few days since she got stung, and I want to check in. I want to see her.

She hobbles back to her table after she lets me in. "Is your foot still numb, or do you just want attention?"

"A little."

"You just want a little attention?"

"That, too."

I laugh, try not to look at her messy bed, begging for a body to climb back into it. Two bodies. "Everybody is headed out today. Call me when you're done working and we can get out of here for a while, too, if you want."

"Where is everyone going?"

"Dice has got a tournament. Josephine is headed back to Albuquerque in a few hours. Cujo is going wherever he goes. Says he'll be gone for a few weeks. Petra, Myrna, and the spooky sisters are all taking off together for the weekend. No seasonal residents are scheduled to come back over the next few days, so it's probably Petra's last chance to get away before somebody needs something from her. Mine, too, honestly. But I don't have any plans."

"So, for the next few days, you and I will be the only ones in Ivydell?"

"Yeah."

"Are you out here alone a lot?"

"Not a lot."

"Do strange things ever happen when everyone else leaves?"

"Yeah. It gets pretty weird. Wild animals invade. Ghosts appear everywhere. UFOs hover. Thousands of them. You probably shouldn't be alone."

"Which one of us needs attention?"

"Me. But I'm going to get out of here so you can work. Let me know when you're done, and we'll go do something."

"Oh, sure, just drop in to tease me and then leave me hanging."

"You need to work."

"You're not wrong." She glances at her phone to check the time. "I'll be done in about three hours."

"Sounds good."

I have fuck all to do for the next three hours. Might as well do it right.

Dice finds me in my Adirondack chair, staring at nothing.

Thinking about everything. I hear him pull up and hope for a minute that it's Ivy, but I know it's too soon. He calls out as he comes around the corner. "What are you doing out here?"

"Nothing. Sitting and thinking."

"It's the thinking that'll get you in trouble." He laughs and sits in the chair next to me.

I guess he's not quite ready to pull out of the gate yet. "You want a beer?"

"No. Just not looking forward to getting on the road again."

"You worried about the tournament or just the trip?"

"She's playing again."

"Your ex?"

"Yep."

"First time you've seen each other in how long?"

"Six years."

"Who won?"

"Wasn't me."

"You worried about her game or her?"

"She is her game."

"There are people who worry about your game."

"Yeah, but she ain't one of them. Mind if I sit here and do nothing with you for a while?"

"Not at all."

I wonder what the odds are of there being two ex-spouses playing in any other poker tournament this weekend. Not that I'm any good at calculating odds. But I think about them a lot, how they're obviously stacked against some people, and how others think their chances are so much better than they are. The odds of a car accident in the rain aren't slim. All three occupants of the same car being killed is a bigger longshot, but it can happen. Nothing is a sure thing.

We sit and stare, mutter something of no importance to each other occasionally. Until he says, "I've been hearing about this cute redhead out here taking up all your downtime. Why are you all alone today?"

The mere mention of her lifts my mood. "She had to work today. I'm seeing her when she's done."

"I also heard she's only staying a few months. That's a big smile on your face for a temporary thing."

"Ice cream's temporary, but I don't think I've ever been pissed off about eating it."

"That's deep, man. You should write a book." He laughs at me, and I don't mind. His mood is better now, too.

"For all you know, that's why I'm here. I could be writing a book about you."

"Make me look good, that's all I ask."

"Don't worry. You'll be a winner."

"From your lips to God's ears." He stands to go, and his eyes widen at the sound of Ivy's car pulling up. "I think your ice cream is being delivered."

"Fuck you." I shake his hand with the smile still on my face. "Have a good weekend."

"Hey, you, too." He looks around at the dirt and scrub we've been looking at for too long already. "Thanks for your help today."

He could mean thanks for helping him with the water heater, but I think he meant something else. "Anytime."

I walk up front with him and introduce him to Ivy.

When he drives away, she says, "Did he call me ice cream when he said goodbye?"

"Did he?" I shrug. "He says weird shit, sometimes."

"I saw Josephine leave earlier, and Myrna's shock-mobile wasn't there when I left. Is everyone else gone already?"

"It's just me and you."

"What should we do?" Her eager smile is already doing things to me. She's always doing things to me without even trying.

I pin her against her car. "Got any outdoor fantasies? Are you a closet exhibitionist, Ivy?"

The hard way she swallows makes me think the answer is yes, but she laughs and says no. I press my forehead to hers and look into her clear eyes. "Are you sure? If I slipped my hand into your panties, I wouldn't find you wet at the thought of being taken right here?"

"We're too close to the gate. What if someone came back because they forgot something?"

"Maybe the thought of getting caught is what makes it hot." I cup her pussy through her leggings.

"No," she says. "Not right out in the open like this. It's only hot if you're at least partially hidden, some place secluded enough that the odds of getting caught are lower, even if they're not zero."

I like our odds right here, but I like the thought of her being into it way more. "Where would that place be?"

"If we happen upon it, I'll let you know."

She playfully pushes against my chest. I back up and pull her in for a hug. My heartbeat thuds, and I try not to think about her being ice cream. "You want to go get something to eat?"

"Do I have to change clothes?"

"Not for the place I'm thinking of."

"Then yes, feed me."

"It's over an hour away. Do you need a snack for the road?"

"Are you offering to make me popcorn again?"

"I'm offering you a bag of chips."

"Fine. I accept your offer."

I had a feeling she might. She forgets to eat when she's working. Releasing our hug, I'm struck by how comforting it is to know a minor detail like that about her. Not that I like the fact that she skips meals, but I'm glad I know.

She comes inside with me to get her chips.

"Do you need to pee before we leave?"

"No, mommy. I already went." Her voice is pure sass. She snatches the bag of chips from me with a smirk and walks toward the door.

I come up behind her and smack her ass before she makes it back outside. "You mispronounced Daddy." She sucks in a quick breath, and her head whips around, revealing a wry smile that makes me want to spank her for real.

We've gotten to know each other quickly, but I have a feeling we might be on the verge of learning a lot more.

She takes bites from her potato chips instead of putting the whole thing in her mouth. The way she crunches on them while she keeps talking is cute. Nothing about her annoys me. I wasn't even annoyed by her when we met and I pretended to be. I just didn't want the distraction of her. The temptation. Right now, I want to kiss her and taste the salt on her lips. I fucking always want to kiss her.

"I guess I should've asked if you're okay with barbecue."

"Oh, my God. I haven't had barbecue in forever. Of course, I'm okay with that. As long as it's good barbecue."

"Are you doubting my tastebuds?"

"Maybe a little."

"You'll see."

It's early enough that the parking lot is only mostly full when we get there. I watch her check out the old building as we pull in. She reads the claim painted on the side. "Ranked fourth best barbecue in the state by Texas Monthly. What year?"

What year! "Haven't you ever heard you shouldn't judge a book by its cover? The building may not look like much, but they deserve that ranking. It should probably be higher."

I love that she actually eats instead of just picking at her food. And I could watch her suck barbecue sauce off her fingertips all day long. It might eventually give me a heart attack, but I'd die happy. The way she tips back a longneck beer bottle is sexier than it has a right to be. Every time she takes a drink, I remember her on her knees with only a towel to cushion them.

I've never been disappointed by this place, but I can honestly say this is the first time my dick's gotten hard in a booth here.

We decide to share a slice of pecan pie for dessert. Well, she decides, but I'm totally fine with the choice. She and the server exchange a silent giggle after I order it. "Why do I feel like you and that woman have an inside joke?"

"Because you asked for pee-khan pie."

"I can't say puh-khan. It's never going to sound right to me."

"You can say it however you want. It's cute."

"Cute? Okay." I watch her drain the rest of her bottle. "No matter how you say it, this is the only place I've ever seen people wash it down with beer."

"Eh, to be fair, it doesn't sound like it would go together as well as it does."

"What's your favorite food?"

"Seafood." She sighs. "I know, girl from the coast loves seafood. I'm a cliché."

"I love seafood, too, but that's a broad category."

"I like it all. Except razor clams. Blech." She makes a yuck face. "They're chewy."

"I've actually had razor clams, and they were definitely not chewy. I think you ordered them at the wrong place."

"I'll take your word for it because I'm never ordering them again."

"Wow. Not big on second chances, huh?"

"Nope. Get it right the first time or get the fuck out." She laughs. "Okay, I'm not really that harsh."

"I bet you can hold a grudge."

"Only when it's deserved."

"Anyone in particular come to mind?"

"The man who fathered me."

"Commonly referred to by some people as simply their father."

"Those people can probably put a face to the title."

"Damn. I'm sorry."

"Don't be. I have it on good authority that he was a loser, and my mom and I were both better off without him."

"You close to your mom?"

"Yeah. She and Gran raised me."

"I think they did a good job."

"Thanks. It seems like whoever raised you did pretty well, too."

"Both parents. I survived, so I guess it could've been worse." My stomach clenches. "You ready to get out of here?"

"I've eaten everything but the salt shaker, so, yeah. I think I've done all the damage I can do here."

"Was this the first thing you've eaten all day?"

"No. I had some chips earlier." She winks at me as she slides out of the booth. "I need to pee before we leave."

Her smart-ass sense of humor disarms me. The woman has probably charmed her way out of everything from arguments to speeding tickets. Smart. Funny. Beautiful.

Ice cream, I remind myself. Temporary.

I start my truck but don't put it in reverse yet. "Hey, just so we're clear, when I made the daddy comment earlier, I wasn't saying I thought you had daddy issues."

"Oh," she says. "So, apparently, I'm the one who needs to clarify things here. A woman can have a daddy *kink* without having daddy *issues*, and I only have the former. They are two entirely separate things. Maybe some women have both, but I just have the one."

I'd back us out of this parking spot now if I could remember how to drive. There's a shortage of blood in my brain at the moment. It all rushed straight to my dick as soon as the words daddy and kink left her perfect mouth together.

Ice cream, dude. She might be your favorite goddamn flavor, but she's still ice cream.

Ivy

Exploring in the Dark

IVYDELL LOOKS THE SAME when we get back, but it feels different knowing we are the only two people here. I still haven't seen the whole place. It's dark, but I'm curious where all the casitas are situated and how much open land is inside the fence.

"Can you show me all of Ivydell? I've only seen as far as Petra's."

"Yeah. I can't believe you haven't driven around and checked it out." He keeps driving past his casita and around the curve that leads to mine.

"I was afraid I'd get lost or someone I hadn't met yet would see me and mistake me for a trespasser."

"We don't get a lot of trespassers. They probably would've just assumed you were new, and either introduced themself or reached out to Petra about you. You wouldn't have gotten shot or any-thing."

"I know that now, but at first, I felt like I shouldn't wander around too much on my own."

The casitas get farther apart. Some rows have only one or two, and then there's a wide-open area with none. "Is that it? Is it just vacant land from here?"

"No, we haven't gotten to Shadow's yet."

"Wow. He's way back here." It's amazing how much you can

see with no streetlights. The moon and stars are so much brighter here than they are at home. Jensen's headlights wash over a large ring of rocks. There's a round concrete picnic table in the center. No matching benches are next to it, but there are long wooden benches placed in rows, almost like church pews. "What's that?"

"That's the circle. It gets used for demonstrations, mostly during the festival."

"What gets demonstrated?"

He raises his eyebrows suggestively. "No one told you about the sacrifices?"

"I was told they only happen on full moons." I stare at the makeshift amphitheater. "This is where we should've watched the meteor shower."

"You're right." He parks and shuts off the engine. "I didn't even think of coming over here for that. But since we're here now, do you want to get out and look at the stars?"

"What a great idea. How'd you come up with it?"

"I'm a hopeless romantic. It just came to me."

"I'll buy the hopeless part."

I like when he laughs at my mean jokes. He's definitely secure enough to handle the occasional jab. He can dish them out, too, and I like that he does, that he isn't too careful around me. Nothing about him feels fake.

We step over the rock perimeter to enter the circle, and he takes my hand and leads me toward the center. He sits on the table. I stand in front of him, admiring his silhouette against a starry sky background. "Seriously, what type of demonstrations happen here?"

"So much nudity. Debauchery. Depravity."

"So much for seriousness."

"What if I was serious?"

"If you want to see me naked in the moonlight, maybe you should just ask."

"Take off your clothes."

"That sounded more like a command."

"Your inaction is reading like disobedience."

"What if I get stung by another scorpion?"

He stands up and runs the sole of his boot back and forth over the ground. His eyes glimmer when he cocks his head and says, "I cleared you a spot. Be a good girl and stay right here, and you won't get stung."

I step into the area he's brushed for me. He reclaims his seat on the table and smiles.

Backing away from a dare has never been my style. I'll take off my clothes, but I'm not stripping for him. It's chilly out here, and there are so many bigger reasons that this could be a bad idea: scorpions, badgers, mountain lions . . . At least it's too cold for rattlesnakes. I think.

I step out of my shoes and take off my socks. "I better not regret this."

"Regret's a waste of time." He holds out his hands for my shoes and socks and sets them on the table next to him.

Shimmying out of my leggings, I lift one foot and then the other to free them. They land on top of my shoes when I toss them at the table. I pull my sweater over my head and add it to the pile. My bra joins, and then my panties.

"No objection about my lack of artistic performance?"

"Were you trying to antagonize me?" His question hits like a warning, and I pull my shoulders up against the cool temps settling on them. "Relax. Hold still."

"You want me to stand here on display for you?"

"Yes. That's exactly what I want."

The chill in the air contracts my nipples to the point of aching, but there's a warmth in my core that spreads at the sound of his deepened voice.

"Why?"

"Because you're going to leave too soon, and I'll want to recall every inch of you."

"You plan on staying here forever?"

"I had no long-term plans when I arrived. Still don't. Some days it feels more temporary than others. More often than not lately."

"Where would you go if you left?"

"Don't know yet. Maybe that's why I'm still here."

His eyes continue to roam over me as we talk, but I feel more adored than scrutinized. Though I know he definitely intends the power dynamic at play, I'm not being demeaned, just dominated a little. I can get onboard with that. Hell, I can get off on that. Obviously, so can he.

I lift my hair off my shoulders, fan it out, and let it fall. He doesn't chide my movement. "Is this the only part of Texas you've seen?"

"Pretty much."

"In four years?"

"Haven't felt like doing a lot of traveling."

Dozens of questions queue up on my tongue, but they're all too personal to ask. Not just because we're in Ivydell, but because I don't know him well enough to ask what upended his life to bring him here, why he'd sell a winery meant to be his and hide away from the world. What was he running from? Why is he still hiding? He's not an artist or a medium or an outlaw, as far as I can tell. Only an outsider by choice. There's too much charisma there for him to have sought this place without something traumatic driving him to it.

I cup my breasts in my hands, both to turn him on and warm me up. He leans forward and watches intently as I knead them, pinch and pull my nipples. How much longer before he'll touch me? Is it a game? A battle of will?

One hand glides down my body to stroke my pussy.

"Hold it open. Show me that pretty little snatch."

Forced vulnerability.

I wonder whose resolve is weakened more by it.

My teeth dig into my bottom lip because it might be mine.

His eyes rake over me with increased hunger. "Turn around. Let me see all of you."

With my back to him, I lift my hair again, leaning my head back as I let it fall, ensuring the ends brush lower, knowing I control his gaze with the motion.

The soft sound of his boots meeting the dirt makes my back arch further. He fists my hair, pulls my head back a few more inches, and looks into my eyes as he leans down to kiss me.

"Bend over the table. Palms flat and tilt that gorgeous ass up for me."

He doesn't start with a gentle slap. The first strike leaves a sting. A warm, oh, so welcome sting. I whimper at the next one, and he massages over where he's spanked for a few seconds before he spanks me again. My eyes well with tears that roll down my cheeks when I blink. It's not the pain; it's the release of it.

His hand slides between my legs, and he slips two fingers into my seam, moving them up and back, spreading my juices. An appreciative groan lingers before he says, "Do you need to be spanked some more?"

Before I can answer, his body is hunched over mine, his mouth right beside my ear when he asks, "Or do you want something else?"

"Yes."

"Yes, what?"

"Something else. I want you inside me."

He presses his fingers into my pussy. "Like this? Is this what you want inside you?"

They feel good, but we both know I need more. "I want you to fuck me. I need to be filled with every inch of your dick."

"Ask me nicely."

"Please." I look over my shoulder. "Please, Daddy."

The familiar sound of his zipper prompts my walls to clench. As the swollen tip fills my opening, I close my eyes and try to memorize the feeling of him pushing into me so I can recall every inch when this is all a memory.

I reach down to my clit, and his hand follows to cover mine. He doesn't take over or change the way I touch it, just rests his hand gently on top to feel what I'm doing. His dick swells inside me as my hand circles faster.

"Yeah, there you go. Make it feel right, baby. Come all over my dick like Daddy's good little whore." The strain in his voice sounds immense, but he keeps his pace steady. He doesn't change a thing while my orgasm builds. He waits until I gasp and come all over his dick, just like he told me to, before he fucks me harder, chasing his own release.

He grips my hip hard with one hand while the other folds over my opposite shoulder as he slams into me, fucking me in this ceremonial circle like he owns me. I'm on the balls of my feet when he comes. The force of his final thrusts steals my breath, leaving us both panting over the table.

A long, rattling hiss sounds from somewhere close. It reverberates down the back of my neck. "Is that a rattlesnake?"

"No. It's just a Burrowing Owl. They mimic rattlesnakes. Our sounds must've scared it, so it's trying to scare us back. Rattlers aren't active yet. It's still too cold."

"Are you sure?"

"Mostly."

He zips his pants awfully fast for a man who's mostly sure. "Grab your clothes. I've got you."

I gather my things from the table, and he lifts my feet off the ground, cradling me in his arms as he carries me to the truck.

When I sort through my clothes on my lap, he says, "You don't need to put anything back on."

"Okay." I set everything close enough to be within easy reach.

He drives us deeper onto the property. There are some mesquite trees back here, lots of native shrubs and more cactus types—overall, more cover for animals. Realizing this makes me anxious.

"That's Shadow's place."

It's looks smaller than the other casitas, but that may just be a byproduct of my heightened wariness back here. I never knew owls could make a sound like that, and I'm still unsure about it.

I don't bother with my bra, but I pull my sweater back on. It's not logical, but a layer between me and the wildlife helps. The warmth and softness are soothing.

Jensen looks over and grins. "God, you're sexy."

"Fear of rattlesnakes must look good on me. It must be the adrenaline rush."

"You always look good."

"Is the meteor shower still going on?"

"No. I saw it, too. That was a falling star."

"Did you make a wish?"

"You can have mine. Make two wishes."

I close my eyes and make the same wish twice.

Jensen

Making Plans

I wake up to Ivy shaking me. "I've got it!" she repeats.

"Got what?"

"The name for your casita."

"And you just couldn't wait to tell me?"

"Well, obviously. We probably don't have long before everyone comes back, and the surreal peace of the past few days will be gone. It won't feel like we're the only two people left alive anymore."

"So, we need to be extra alive between now and then?"

"Yes, wake up. Let's be extra alive."

I sit up and try to blink myself awake. "You know, some people would just want to enjoy their last few hours of surreal peace."

"Scorpion's Sting!"

It takes me a minute to make the connection. Oh, that's the name she's come up with.

"No. That's a negative thing. Why would I want to live in a place named after something painful?"

"It's perfect. I'm going to make a sign, and then it'll be official."

"That's not how it works."

"Why are you fighting me on this? You don't even care that it doesn't have a name, so why would you care what the name is?"

"I like it better without a name."

"Scorpion's Nest?"

"No. You're going to have to come up with something with better vibes."

She drags the blanket off the bed and wraps it around her shoulders.

"Hey! Where are you going with my blanket?"

"Outside to sit in your staring chairs. Come join me." She slides open my back door. "Bring coffee."

I stumble out of bed and pull on a pair of sweats. Her hair is blowing in the wind, and she's wearing nothing but my blanket. I've never seen an Adirondack chair look better.

I'll make her coffee, but she's getting eggs, too.

"Here's your coffee." She breaks her trance and smiles at me as she takes the mug. "And here's your breakfast."

She looks into the bowl of scrambled eggs with cheese and hatch chiles. "I'm not really a breakfast person."

"You are today."

"Okay, but only because chewing helps me think."

Sure, it's not the actual food that activates your brain, it's just the chewing part.

The blanket slips off her shoulder. Her hair's a mess, and her eyes are still swollen from sleep. She takes a bite of her eggs, followed by a sip of her coffee. "Mmmm. Why does everything you put in my mouth always taste so good?"

Maybe I'll let her name my place after all.

She realizes what she's said and cracks up at herself. "You know what I meant. Your wine, your picnic food, the fourth best barbecue in the state, and now this? All good stuff."

"I pride myself on offering the good stuff. Wine, food, vibes, sex

. . ."

Coffee dribbles from her mouth when she tries to speak before she's swallowed her last sip. "That's it! Vintage Vibes!"

She nods her head vigorously, like if she does it long enough, I'll catch on.

"This place is old, so it's vintage. You know wine, and that's a different type of vintage. The place gives good vibes, and so do you. Voila! Vintage Vibes."

"I guess I could live with that."

"Yay! At least I'll know after I'm gone there will be something here to remind you of me."

"First of all, everything is going to remind me of you. Second of all, I'm not under house arrest here, you know? And once you leave, you're not banished. There's no reason we couldn't keep seeing each other."

"You mean like . . . do the long-distance thing?"

"Maybe. Why not? We've still got some time to make up our minds, but I don't see why we shouldn't be open to it."

"So, you might feel like doing a little traveling, huh?"

"I think I might." I sit on the arm of her chair, take a bite of her eggs, and then feed her a bite.

Six more weeks together doesn't seem like much time, but I've only known her for two and it feels like a lifetime—or the start of one. The start of something, anyway.

It wouldn't be so bad to give this place a name. Something for people to remember me by after I've moved on to wherever I go next. I'm still deciding what comes next for me.

But I don't envision myself alone everywhere anymore.

"Quit eating all my eggs." She takes the fork away from me.

I hear Cujo's bike rolling on the main road like thunder. He was supposed to be gone for weeks.

That's the thing about plans: you can always make them, but you can't always keep them from changing.

Book 2 in the Ivydell series:

Shit Happens in Ivydell

ebook available from Amazon
paperback available from your favorite book retailers

Welcome back to Ivydell!

Ivy and Stinger are no longer fighting their feelings, though they're both still trying to avoid thinking about what happens when her time in Ivydell is up. As the community gears up for the annual festival and more seasonal residents return, there is plenty happening to keep them occupied--not to mention the sizzling happenings between them that definitely keep them fully present.

Can two people so skilled at keeping their distance handle getting so close so fast? Will the new wear off? What if the sight of Jensen shirtless stops causing a tingling sensation in her core? What if her cropped shirts and tight leggings stop making his calloused fingers ache to feel her softness?

It's not like there's love potion in the water or the desert air or scorpion venom. Ivydell is just another quirky place.

Right?

Also from INDIE SPARKS

Steamy Rom-Com Duologies

VENGEFUL VIXENS:
Your Boss Says Hi!

She's only looking for a rebound guy, but her ex's boss plays for keeps. He's a former NFL player who used to have thousands of women screaming his name every week. Now, he only wants one woman to scream his name, and she just might become his biggest fan yet.

Your Trainer Says Hi!

She only wants to see her ex's beloved personal trainer in the gym—until he convinces her his hot tub could do wonders for her aching muscles. He isn't wrong, but between the heat, the bubbles, and his off-the-clock skills, she might be in too deep before she knows it. He's definitely not her type. So, why can't she stop seeing him?

NAUGHTY AT THE NOUVEAU:

Maintenance & Management

She's the new property manager. He's the new maintenance supervisor. They rub each other the wrong way . . . until they start to rub each other so very right. There's a non-fraternization policy, so they really shouldn't. But there's only one bed!

Landscaping & Leasing

He ghosted her after an unfortunate incident that she had absolutely no control over—and now, she's accidentally hired his landscaping company. She may not be completely immune to his charms (that voice!), but she's not weak enough to fall for him twice. But what if she doesn't know the whole story about why he disappeared from her life?

Thank you, intrepid readers!

Thank you for taking a chance on this cartoon cover book with words like "hippie-dippy" used in its marketing materials and posts. It's not lost on me that your interest may have been piqued more by words like "scorpion tattoo" and "shirtless." You are clearly ruled by curiosity, and I love that about you. I trust that Jensen Stinger did not disappoint.

Thank you also for not being deterred by this being the first book in a four-book series. I hope you are looking forward to the next book as much as I'm looking forward to sharing it with you.

Kayleigh, thank you for continuing to wrangle my behind-the-scenes author life, making sure my newsletter goes out and ARCs get distributed, allowing me more time to write, and occasionally even shower and leave the house.

Speaking of ARCs, thank you to everyone on my team and those who read an advance copy provided through BCAT. Your early interest in this book meant the world. I will always be thankful when you make time for my stories.

Special thanks to Christy and Darcy for saying from the first promo graphic how much you were looking forward to this one, and for all the cheerleading on past books. Your enthusiastic emojis and GIFs so often put a much-needed smile on my face.

Merri, thanks for always asking about my books, for your encouragement, and for sharing the good, the bad, and the WTF-ery of the Day with me, whether we need to laugh, rage or cry about it. Thank you for your friendship. It continues to be a bright spot in an ever-changing world.

To my fellow admins in the Cinnamon Roll Book Boyfriends group on Facebook: Wow! It's crazy to think we were strangers not so long ago. I'm in awe of your talent, knowledge, and generous spirits. From someone who typically hates chats, I sincerely thank you for the chats.

Beth, from throwing some pizazz on my name, to walking me through technical steps on my lovely website you created until you probably gave me just enough skills to be dangerous, to editing my words . . . I want you to know I appreciate you. And I like you, too. Thanks for being such a likeable pro. → That's Beth Hudson, Ink, y'all!

And forever, thanks, Mr. Sparks! I'm sorry you didn't realize being my assistant at a book signing was not a one-time event, but a permanent assignment. What can I say? Marriages evolve, babe.